ALSO BY BRIAN KITELEY

Still Life with Insects

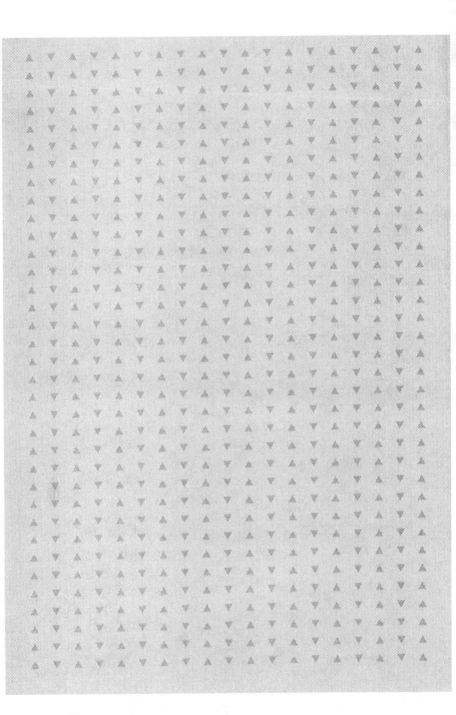

I Know
Many Songs,
but I Cannot
Sing

BRIAN KITELEY

SIMON & SCHUSTER

New York   London   Toronto

Sydney   Tokyo   Singapore

Simon & Schuster
Rockefeller Center
1230 Avenue of the Americas
New York, NY 10020

Designed by Jeanette Oleander
Manufactured in the United States of America

10 9 8 7 6 5 4 3 2 1

Library of Congress Cataloging-In-Publication Data
Kiteley, Brian.
I know many songs, but I cannot sing / Brian Kiteley.
p. cm.
1. City and town life—Egypt—Cairo—Fiction.
2. Americans—Travel—Egypt—Cairo—Fiction.   I. Title.
PSS3561.I855115   1996
813..54—dc20   95-44900   CIP
ISBN: 0-7432-3759-5

For information regarding the special discounts for bulk purchases, please contact Simon
Schuster Special Sales at 1-800-456-6798 or business@simonandschuster.com

Most loving thanks to
Cynthia, reader, editor, extra set of
eyes and ears.

I would also like to thank
Allen Hibbard, Nora Thompson
Hibbard, Eli Gottlieb, Tom Andrews,
and Mark Sedgwick. I wrote this
book in part on postcards to dozens
of friends and family members. I
appreciated everyone's forbearance.
I wish to acknowledge the generous
support of the John Simon Guggen-
heim Memorial Foundation, the
National Endowment for the Arts,
and the Fine Arts Work Center in
Provincetown.

This novel is dedicated to
the memory of my brother Geoffrey.

A confidence man learns early in his career that to commit himself to paper is to court trouble.

GEOFFREY WOLFF

Ib STILL MISREADS SIMPLE images: the shadow cast by a sleeping child is the family cat back home in Massachusetts snuggling illogically into the ribs of this dusty Egyptian kid halfway around the world. Jet lag, dehydration. A young Egyptian man joins him at the same pace, walking too close for Ib's comfort and on his deaf side. He says, *"Vous voulez un bateau?"* Ib has lived in Cairo three years, but he's still a tourist to the local touts. Tourists ride the lateen sailboats on the Nile. Ib flew to Massachusetts four days ago for his stepfather's funeral and returned this morning. He usually answers in Arabic, "I am *not* a foreigner," which often confuses these people. But today he shakes his head and sleepwalks over the uneven flagstones and gazes up at a lovely mixture of date palms and feather-leaved locust trees. The fight with his oldest sister after the funeral replays itself. She called Ib a *foreigner.* There were divided loyalties when his parents divorced and, after their mother divorced their Dutch stepfather, remarried each other. Ib's sister felt he grieved too ostentatiously over his stepfather, and that this was a veiled criticism of their parents' remarrying. But *foreigner* was such an odd thing to call Ib that a bubble of silence followed the word. Then both siblings burst out laughing; hugs, kisses, tension reduced but not entirely eliminated. "I am not a foreigner," Ib repeats to himself in Arabic. *Ana mish khawaga.*

Time passes, and Ib is amid the African jungle aromas of a nursery that impolitely obstructs a public promenade with basket ferns and rubber trees and passion flowers. He finds himself in conversation with the fellow who asked if he wanted a boat ride. Ib does not speak French well but soon is chattering away in it, relieved to be speaking a language so similar to English (and weary after an hour of conversation in Arabic with his tutor). It is perfect spring weather, warm and dry, the air pollution blown briefly into the desert, and the odors of unwashed bodies and donkey manure and absolutely unregulated vehicle exhaust fumes are as intoxicating as ever. Without being asked, Ib tells his

companion that he is an American teaching Middle East-
ern history to Egyptian students in an English-language
university. The Egyptian does not laugh. He tells Ib that
he teaches, too, at a secondary school called Dar es
Salaam near the Palace of the President. Ib knows *dar
es salaam* means the realm of peace, where Islam is as-
cendant (as opposed to the realm of war, *dar el harb,*
where it is not). The Egyptian says, "I am Gamal. We
will be good friends," and Ib wants to believe this common rhetorical flourish. But when Ib asks where the
city of Dar es Salaam is, their continents begin to drift
apart. The city is somewhere in Africa and for the moment this feels to Ib like the missing piece of a puzzle.
In answer, Gamal describes in great detail how his
school building is laid out. He finishes and asks, "*Compris? C'est compris?*" Ib says yes but that Gamal has misunderstood his question, so he rephrases it. Again the
elaborate architectonic tale; it seems Gamal wants to
become an architect in Paris. All this Ib learns, almost
against his will, but he cannot make himself understood
on one small point. Where is Dar es Salaam? Gamal
says (in English with a French accent), "You say you
comprehend, then you say you don't. I can't comprehend what you fail to comprehend." Ib loses that dim
glow of fellow feeling, and he asks with irritation, "You

told me you teach, so why did you ask if I wanted a ride in a *bateau?*" Gamal says he was translating for a boy whom Ib did not seem to hear. Despite Ib's deaf ear, this answer fills him with distrust. They stop by the banyan tree in front of the Indian Embassy, and Gamal feebly asks for Ib's phone number, which Ib honestly cannot remember. The ministry of communication changed it last week. An Egyptian military policeman sits half asleep in his narrow booth with an unloaded rifle on his shoulder. *"Bien,"* Gamal says, wheeling around, insulted Ib has not offered the hospitality of his home or even his telephone after Gamal was so generous with his talk, his time, his work, and his afternoon promenade. He disappears. Dar es Salaam is the capital of Tanzania, Ib remembers, with a slap of the forehead. When he is sure Gamal is gone, Ib turns around and retraces his steps along the Nile half a mile to his apartment building. His sisters saw him off at the airport, and his middle sister said mildly, "You loved your stepfather more than your own father." Except Ib had heard, "More than your own fatherland," and when he found the remark hilarious, his sisters just stared at him.

▲ ▼ ▲ ▼ ▲ ▼ ▲ ▼ ▲ ▼ ▲

Egypt is a green and black lotus when viewed from the upper atmosphere, cleanly chopped off at the Aswan High Dam and set in the earthen vase of Lake Nasser. Nutrients steadily bleed from the enormous flower. The Nile no longer floods annually and the soil grows saltier each year. Cairo is the knot at the point in the plant where stalk becomes flower—a tumor that now threatens to choke off this ancient organism. The river ran a few miles east several centuries ago, so the modern colonial city of high-rise hotels and government bureaucracy stands in old riverbed and swampland. Examine one small part of medieval Cairo, which sits on higher ground on the former banks of the Nile. A certain street can't make up its mind which direction to go and dithers, turning sharply here and there, narrowing, then widening, before it abruptly concludes in a great pile of bricks and trash. As if it were a mountainside, goats perch on this ruin of a once fashionable caravanserai, an old hotel for camels and men. A dozen steps from this rubble, the second floor of a three-story building juts out over half the lane. Peeling turquoise paint reveals faded yellow beneath. Ib dangles for a moment outside a window in this boxy section of the building. He grips the wooden latticework of the build-

15

ing across the street, only two feet away at this height, to stare in at the room from which he has just crawled. In the apartment is another man named Gamal, thin and wiry with a nearly implausible shock of black hair like the first Gamal Ib had met halfway across this big city earlier in the day. When he met the second Gamal in front of a perfume merchant's shop near Husseyn Square, Ib asked him if they had run into each other that afternoon in Zamalek. The man misunderstood the question and spoke for a time about his brother, who works at the Safeway in Zamalek. Ib lands on the hard-packed earth floor of the alley, and two boys fly by shouldering hot metal pans of bubbling eggplant casserole from the neighborhood's communal ovens. They pay him no heed. The smell that lingers in their path briefly blurs the scenery. It is Ramadan, fifteen minutes before sunset, when the city will break its daylight fast.

Ib studies the area for a place to hide and to stake out the apartment he's just left. A hill of shoes sits in the middle of the dirt street. The sagging buildings are two and three stories, with evidence of grandeur in the elaborately carved entry doors, but the top floors are newer, shoddier, lamed by too much sand in the concrete. The confusion of line and color across the way coalesces into meaning: a barbershop. Ib enters and takes the only chair, waving his right hand to prevent a haircut. He asks in a whisper if they mind him sitting here for a few minutes. The puzzled barber nods graciously, and his tiny malnourished son returns to poking the single pot of *fuul* cooking on a hot plate in the corner of the cavelike space. The smell of burnt garlic and turmeric sends a wave of calm through Ib's frazzled nervous system. All three people in the small room are disoriented from lack of food and grateful for the promise of something in their stomachs. The barber and his son accept the foreigner's strange behavior because during this last week of Ramadan it's normal to be inside out and upside down, sleepy during the daylight fast, eating the biggest meal at midnight, and awake before dawn for a light snack and prayers.

In the apartment above the street, Gamal carries a tray from the kitchen to the only other room, which has a sleeping mat and a low table with candles on it. The tray holds two tiny glasses, a brass *kanaker* of steaming Turkish coffee, and a cellophane tube of Biscomisr cookies with which to break the fast. This is not the usual *iftar*, which would be the glass of dates and water, the cup of tea. Gamal is still talking nonstop, as he has been since they met in Husseyn Square an hour before. Gamal does not yet know that Ib is missing. Ib climbed out of Gamal's home to escape this maddening talk. So why is Ib spying on this man's movements after his clean getaway? Ib behaved rudely by sneaking off without saying goodbye or thanking Gamal for the hospitality. But Gamal was equally ill-mannered. Ib does not know why he is watching this man.

Some of the subjects covered during Gamal's hour of talk: the great friendship they will have; the difficulty Gamal has accepting Ib's name—he prefers to call him Ibrahim; the movies of Kaleemt Ishtwud; the language of Arabic, which Gamal will make Ib speak like one good Arab Man, which Gamal says is the language everyone in the world knows; felucca rides on the Nile; the English language, the greatest language on earth, which Ib will teach Gamal to speak like one good English Man; this great beauty the singer Paula Abdul, but what is she a servant of (abdul means "servant of") and how can we make her visit our house which we will build together near the Pyramids; the Pyramids, which Gamal feels one moment are the great monuments of the world we know, the next moment, garbage heaps, where bad people sell bad things that do not make Egypt look good; the right of a man to marry a woman for a few weeks, a very necessary right, men are much stronger and fairer this way, men grow beards more quickly, men walk in straight lines.

One detail puzzles Ib. In the middle of these schemes and harangues, Gamal stepped out of character to speak of a recent Egyptian novel, which had been serialized in the Communist newspaper *Al-Ahali*. Ib keeps track of such things, and he had not heard of the book, nor the writer. Gamal's review of the novel was entertaining. A sultan in medieval times decides a certain sheikh, later a saint, is developing too large a following. The sultan sends agents to do what they must do. The saint assumes several different forms—as a lowly donkey, as a beautiful young woman, and as a wrinkled old man—to fool the agents of the sultan. They are so baffled they are won over and they turn on their master, who in turn has to disguise himself as a street actor and circus performer to escape their vengeance. Ib accepted this fleeting eruption of literacy in a man he assumed was illiterate, because a love of books and old poems is so common in Cairo. The ability to retell this story with flair and an elegant sense of timing kept Ib interested in Gamal long after he might ordinarily have abandoned him.

The barber invites Ib to join him and his son for *iftar,* to break the Ramadan fast. Ib descends slowly from the chair without turning to acknowledge the invitation. He walks out of the shop, whose walls are painted a soft sweet blue. The barber follows Ib to the edge of the turquoise glow the shop gives off, as if to step beyond it into the vaguely defined street—there is no door or wall to separate the barbershop from the city—would rob him of his powers to speak, to cut hair, to entertain his new friend. Ib tries to ignore the look of sadness that spreads across the globe of the barber's face by examining the shop directly across from this one, dark now, but with a small flame flickering in the corner—a tinsmith, Ib guesses, who keeps a fire going perpetually for heating and molding the tin into shapes and designs dictated by tourism, not utility. He looks up. Ib watches Gamal discover that his very good friend is no longer in the apartment. Ib tells the barber, whose wife probably died in childbirth, that he is very sorry he cannot accept his hospitality. The barber says, "Our feast is only beans and rice without you." Ib walks away, grinning at the barber's wit, making no effort to hide himself from Gamal's view.

He comes around a corner to a street fair. Dozens of people pass him, zombies, walking stomachs. They bump against each other constantly, but never against Ib. The sky is sunlit and daylight blue above the buildings, but it is already dusk in the narrow canyons of these ancient streets. The neighbors have strung a row of blinding halide lights from second-story balconies. Electricity is heavily subsidized by the government so it costs little to waste this way. Children swoop up and down in a boat swing. At one stall, where the object is to shoot at strings of popcorn, the proprietor sits on his tall stool, casually aiming his air rifle at passersby, including Ib. A fly-covered boy is tugging at Ib's shirt. "What time, mister, what time?" Ib usually ignores this question, but there is good reason to want to know the time now: when does the sun set? Without looking at his watch, Ib tells the boy, "Fifteen minutes, better hurry." The boy breathes on both palms and wipes imaginary sweat from his brow and limps off. At the end of the temporary playground, two long tents with orange, black, and green patterns take up the whole width of the street. Ib has heard somewhere that a Christian neighborhood borders this one, and these Muslims know full well that Egyptian Christians on the way to or from work or market will have to squeeze by the tents, peer into the warm, friendly interiors, and wonder for a moment if their centuries of clinging to an outmoded religion are not, after all, wrongheaded.

Ib chooses the darker, less crowded tent, where three European men in their mid-thirties sit on mats talking softly. A fourth man, Egyptian, sits slightly apart, smiling at his socks. Clearly, the Europeans are converts to Islam. They all wear full beards, white robes, and lace skullcaps. The other tent blazes with light, buzzes with chatter and shouts and laughter, and smells of wonderful food. Ib prefers this tent because only four discreet oil lamps illuminate it. An Egyptian would always choose the crowds and noise and light. In Arabic Ib asks the air between the four Sufis if he might join them. One replies courteously, though not warmly, that he is most welcome. Ib removes his shoes and shakes over his shoulders the *kufiyeh* he has been wearing in the style of a European scarf. The aloofness of these converts appeals to him. The convert desires nothing more than to convince other unbelievers to join him in the realm of peace. But it is nearer still to *iftar*. The excitement and derangement such hunger causes is at a fever pitch. No one expects normal courtesies three weeks into the month of fasting. Ib makes a cozy spot on the rugs, slightly outside the group, and he sees the second Gamal walk by. Gamal stares directly in at Ib, but he does not break his stride, and in the next beat he is gone. In the traces this Gamal leaves in his memory, Ib is not sure which one has just passed, the first or the second Gamal. Something he has not noted before about Gamal's dark curly hair strikes him now: the hair is a wig; the wig was slightly askew.

Ib tries to listen to the phlegmatic conversation these men are having. The language feels German at first, but Ib cannot make himself pay attention. They appear to be talking about food. The perfume of roasting lamb wafts over them, and each man's head moves slightly in the direction the smell is coming from.

The muscles across his chest and his shoulders begin to unkink. Ib turns the house lights down in his mind, to conjure up X, an Egyptian woman he knows from the National Library. He closes his eyes and imagines her lying on a hospital table. A thick white towel protects her modesty. A doctor's pink-gloved hands probe her

damaged ears and mouth. Her eyes are open but un-
blinking. The doctor folds the towel back from one
breast and cups the stiff dark nipple in his hand, which
is familiar with this terrain. The other hand reaches
deep into her mouth and pulls something out: a simple
gold wedding band. Noise from the tent intrudes on
this improbable hospital scene. Ib uncrosses his legs.
One of the Sufis has spoken in English, a moment before, and only now does the question form in Ib's mind:
"You sit on your hands as if at any moment you will
jump up and run away. Yet you entered our tent as
though you were coming home. Why this contradic-
tion?"

Ib stares through his eyelids and takes his time answer-
ing. When he has a ripe paragraph of thought to pluck,
he begins. "I do research at the National Library," he
says in English. "It's a great place. I love it. I miss it. The
problem I guess is, there's a woman who worked there.
A young Egyptian woman, very pretty. Her job was in
the microfilm room, where I do most of my research.
Some of the medieval Persian and Arabic poetry manu-
scripts the library has—they're falling apart. The library
has such an enormous . . . treasure of these things and

they're turning to dust. I never thought much about her. But I began to notice she favored me over other researchers. This can be a lonely city for single European men, unless you're a convert." The converts agree vigorously. "Gradually we became friends. I felt awkward with her, but she was so eager to be my friend, and she knew these books fairly well. At first I wondered if she was literate. No, that's ridiculous, she could *read,* but I just assumed she wasn't literate in the archaic language of these poems. I always underestimate Egyptians that way, their knowledge of great poems. What we would consider esoteric literature in the West—they know by heart. When she microfilmed a poem for me that she knew, she was so happy. I found out, eventually, afterwards, that . . . anyway, nothing happened. We had a cup of coffee once. One cup of coffee. Then she didn't come to work. In two years I've never known her to miss a day. I began to hear stories. The front desk started harassing me. I just got my annual work-study visa renewed. An enormous hassle. They are taking longer and longer checking my identification. I asked about her at the desk. They said she'd been . . . hospitalized. Then my library card is taken from me. Now the interior ministry is calling very politely asking me to stop by, and the appointment is invariably canceled at the last moment, usually after I've been sitting in the waiting room half an hour."

The Sufis seem to have moved closer to Ib when he opens his eyes. He examines them carefully for the first time. Like Ib, they are adept at not talking and staring calmly—as if into him. He feels he has met two of them before, a common suspicion among foreigners in Egypt, and usually true. Ib wants to know what country in Europe these men call home. As a test, he says in Dutch, "We could build our highways in the Netherlands as straight as rulers because the land is so flat, but we deliberately kink them to keep drivers alert." One of the converts laughs for an instant, then looks embarrassed, and translates the thought into German for two of his friends and into Arabic for the fourth, who has the preternatural stillness of a sheikh. After this brief exchange, no one talks. The three who spoke Dutch and German could be from anywhere in northern Europe or Scandinavia. Chanting from the next tent leaks into this one. The ground vibrates, hands pounding the earth. Ib examines the Egyptian man he assumes is the sheikh to measure jealousy or any emotion on his face. But he is the picture of self-abnegation. His tariqa of European converts is enough mortification in itself. Ib imagines this man going home to his wife in a middle-class apartment block in Giza. Would he ever vent his spleen over these dim, showy, flat-footed ex-unbelievers? Would his wife shut the door in their faces and shout to her husband, "They're here! Have you not yet convinced them what a silly mistake they made renouncing their own born cultures and religions? They'll never understand Islam, and they'll certainly never marry any of *my* daughters!"

A cheerful voice from the street calls out several friendly Egyptian Arabic greetings, and the four men in the tent, who have formed a glum semicircle around Ib, sit up straighter and put on bright smiles and edge away from him. Another European, also bearded, but dressed in jeans and a leather jacket, enters the tent, takes his shoes off with his back to them, and trots over to the group. He grasps each Sufi by the upper arm and plants a noisy kiss on each cheek. He banters with every man in a different language. Ib can make out German, Danish perhaps, English sprinkled in here and there, as well as Arabic. The recent arrival moves from one vernacular to another without pause or the gear-changing Ib is used to, even though he knows three languages well. The pastiche of foreign words fills the tent with such goodwill that Ib forgets for a long time that he is being completely ignored. He peers into their breathless, hearty conversation, looking from one face to the next as the talk dances from man to man. He is shoulder to shoulder with them, curious one moment, bored the next, but he feels as if he is an intimate part of the conversation. From time to time the new arrival, who is clearly the real sheikh, even puts his hand on Ib's arm or knee while making a point wholly unrelated to Ib.

But Ib knows he does not exist for these men. They can smell his cynicism and casual refusal to accept the simple truths of their faith. They know without even probing that he is not a candidate for conversion. His pathetic story, which the four Sufis have imparted to their sheikh without, Ib imagines, actually telling it, has nothing to do with their ignoring him. He is simply not of any use to them.

Ib replays his story and finds it truthful and accurate, which surprises him because he felt at the time that he was telling a pack of lies. But a few details are not quite true. Ib has had no problem with the library or the government about his visa. The American University takes care of all his work-visa matters. As a matter of general principle, he should be in trouble. The government ought to be looking into the situation. But, so far as he knows, it is not. He still has easy access to the library. He never took the woman across the street for coffee. Even coffee in a public, outdoor café would be enough to condemn him in Egypt. The appearance of sin is as damning as sin itself. He wants at least the possibility of a guilty conscience. Her savage beating and hospitalization might have been remotely his fault if he had taken her across the street for coffee. He uses the "X" in his interior monologues not to protect her innocence, but because he cannot remember her name. Indeed he is not even sure whether she was beaten up or he misunderstood a stray remark. It might have been her appendix.

He stands up. "Why," he says quietly in English, "do you pretend I don't exist?"

The European in the leather jacket motions for Ib to sit down, the first gesture he has directed at him, which undams a flood of gratefulness in Ib's chest. "Haven't you been listening to us?" the leather-jacketed sheikh asks in English. "We've been talking about your case since I arrived. I am sorry. I thought you understood German."

Ib speaks German almost as well as he speaks Dutch and English. His stepfather grew up in Germany and Holland. Ib is astonished to realize his brain has been scrambling the German the converts were speaking.

The sheikh patiently summarizes their discussion. One of the converts knows someone who knows Ib well, and he also recognized Ib from the Dutch Institute, where Ib has lectured several times. He'd heard the story of the beating. This sends a chill through Ib: How can his improvised lie told only to disorient the moral compasses of these holy men have become common knowledge? The sheikh in the leather jacket confesses that they are more worried by the visa problem, which struck a nerve in them all. He explains how each one of them has a similar story. It is ironic how the nominally Muslim government harasses European converts to Islam. "We sympathize with your plight," he says. "But, as you yourself admit, you were wrong to be seen with this woman in public. Even unbelievers must honor the customs of the country."

Ib's deceptions make him feel argumentative. He chooses to speak German. His stepfather once said German is a good language for yelling at dogs.

"How can you honor something you find repugnant?" he says. "When you return to your homelands, do you honor abortion or the careless pornography of advertising? Do you stomach the ingrained attitude that Western businesses deserve to feed on the markets of the Third World? Do you accept it as your fatherland's right to dump on Egyptian peasants the chemicals and drugs and birth control devices our own countries have long banned?"

The sheikh smiles and extends his hand. "I see that we will have to agree to disagree," he says in English.

Ib takes the hand, not to shake it but to pull some emotion out of this man. Still in German, he says, "I don't agree to disagree. I want to hear you say that it was wrong of this woman's cousin, who is an internationally renowned plastic surgeon, to beat her up so badly that he had to operate on her himself. I want all five of you to admit that the violent defense of honor and virginity is the sign of a backward culture."

The German sheikh tries to free his hand. He suddenly laughs, as if he's just gotten a joke. "You Americans. We

31

don't have the luxury of an objective point of view, as you do, because this is now our home."

The German turns the stranglehold of his hand into a handshake. He says, "Stay with us for *iftar.* Smell the food? I promise we will convert only your stomach."

"Yes," Ib says, rising from his crouch. "I have an errand to run, but I'll be right back. Before the cannon shot. Save me a spot."

Tears cloud his view of the exit, and he stumbles into a wooden post, to which he apologizes in Arabic.

Outside, he climbs over ropes and stoops under posts jammed against crumbling walls and comes to a rare quiet street, the inadvertent gift of these prayer tents, which prevent even Korean midget trucks from roaring and honking down this narrow passage. Beyond the last tent is a café. The chairs and tables take up the whole street. The aromas that emanate from the café— mint tea, *karkaday, shisha* pipe smoke, burnt sugar, and coffee—are hypnotizing. A waiter zigzags from table to table, delivering tall glasses filled with dates and water to the lonely smattering of men in the coffee-house who patiently await the cannon shot from the Citadel that will inform them the sun has set so they can break their fasts. Everyone who has a family should be with them now; these men must be recent immigrants to Cairo from the countryside or some of the estimated one million Egyptians from other parts of the country who spend days and weeks dealing with the monstrous centralized bureaucracy, all the while camping out on streets or in parks. The thread of a mournful amplified chant begins to rise above the distant, diminishing car horns, shifting gears, shouts, and clopping hooves. The sky has grown deep blue. Birds return for *iftar* too. This monthlong celebration is really a tribute to evening—the cool and calm of it in the desert world.

Gamal Number Two sits alone at the edge of the tables, watching Ib carefully, eyes just above his newspaper, like a cartoon spy or private detective. Ib walks straight to the chair beside him and says, "Mind if I make myself comfortable in this here seat, Gamal?" in loud American English. "Or are you the other Gamal?" The Egyptian looks bewildered, but after a moment he meticulously folds the crinkling tissue of his newspaper. Gamal lays a

33

palm on his chest, as a taxi driver does when he tries to charge the tourist rate to a foreigner who does not consider himself a tourist. This gesture puts Ib completely at ease, back in the known world of cardboard cutouts of the Egyptian working class. He considered Gamal an unbearable annoyance half an hour ago but is very happy to see him now. He calls to the waiter for coffee and lupini beans. Casually, as a joke, Ib asks why Gamal is following him.

"I follow you not, *Bey*," Gamal says, in English. "There are many of me in this city. I miss you when you leave my window. But I follow you no. You follow me, *mish kidda?* This is happy good luck we do *iftar* together. You go to this table. I live in this table. Ask all my friends." He speaks to the nearest neighbors, a rapid sentence in Arabic that Ib can only partly translate: "Tell the American professor that a woman . . . four streets of leather." The men at nearby tables burst out laughing. Gamal seems at home on stage. He momentarily lights up, grows more noble, while the laughter washes over him.

"You know I follow another American today," Gamal says again in English, in a tone that indicates he has something to confess. "I do not know why."

34

Ib says he is not American, a lie he commonly uses for anonymity. Americans are more exposed, better liked, and representatives of the place most lusted after by the average Egyptian.

"As you say. This American is rich and own many books and understand our ways and he walked as if he knew the secret of happiness, so I follow him from Boulaq across the bridge to Zamalek, and then to the Gezirah Club, and I try to speak with the guards, who are from my village in the Delta. But you put a man in front of the wealthy and he becomes one of them, a snob, patronizing, better than you. But he's no better, he's worse in fact, a pathetic uniformed lackey who licks the trail these slugs leave on the ground and then thanks them. So I climbed a tree and saw you playing tennis in yellow underwear with a beautiful young woman, calling out to her to raise her racket this way or bend her knees or think of the ball as her friend, and I laughed and laughed until I fell out of the tree."

A shiver runs up Ib's spine, like the shadow of a jet thrown from miles above. Gamal appears to have learned, in the course of one paragraph, to speak fluent, unaccented, and idiomatic English. He has also described with chilling accuracy an earlier portion of Ib's day, four hours before and three miles away from where he met this Gamal in Husseyn Square. Shortly after getting home from the airport, he played his regular Tuesday morning tennis match with the daughter of the Egyptian ambassador to Greece in Zamalek. The game might have looked like a lesson because Ib gave Soha many pointers. "Enough of this charade," Ib says calmly, trying to sound commanding, but falling flat in the last syllable of "charade," which he pronounces pompously in the British fashion. "You work for the government," he says. "I don't know why your department is having me followed. Surely you don't think *I* made love to the girl. Everyone I've talked to knows it was the cousin. My behavior was always honorable. I took her across the street to a little coffeehouse on the Nile and we held hands. Nothing more. I wanted to kiss her, but one knows that sort of thing is out of the question."

Gamal begins to laugh. It is an uncomplicated laugh at first, what Ib would call peasant laughter. Ib hears his own idiotic confession and cringes at the bizarre and progressively less plausible versions of this story bubbling out of him tonight. "Erase all that," he says. "Let me try again."

"Naw, you were doing just fine. I wanna hear more," Gamal says in perfect American English, with the flatness of a Californian ordering a burrito on Venice Beach.

They look at each other as if they have just met.

"Who the hell *are* you?" Ib asks. "What kind of game are you playing on me? Did you think you were having fun with some stupid tourist? Well, you were obviously not what you pretended to be from the moment I met you." He is desperate to salvage even the illusion of understanding from this wildly incomprehensible moment.

Gamal stands up and says in an awesome voice, "Who the fuck are you to criticize my acting?"

The café goes silent. Even the women chatting across the street from second-floor windows freeze mid-gesture. The volume of Gamal's outburst staggers Ib, but also sends a brief spasm of pleasure through his system.

Gamal sits down again and leans over Ib's lap and says, looking straight at Ib but with his eyelids fluttering halfway down his eyes, "I performed that role beautifully," now in neutral, mid-Atlantic English. "You have no idea what a subtle game I was playing. For example, I had never before set foot in the flat I claimed was my home. That was a stroke of genius. How did I know the door would be unlocked and no one would be in? At a glance from the street, I could tell it was a single man's digs. He would be off with family, preparing for *iftar.* It was gorgeous." He breaks off and laughs, eyelids blinking so fast Ib has to look away. "But even that is a lie. A single man's digs! There is no such thing in Cairo, but a callow foreigner like you would not know that. The rooms are rented from an Egyptian family by an English friend of mine who's trying to go native. And what about your so-called acting ability? You have been nothing but a series of insincere and unsuccessful masks since I first saw you. You were a pretentious ass with that girl who tutors you in Arabic. You treated her like some precious porcelain doll whose virginity was the only reason she was so valuable. You weren't slobbering over her like most Europeans would, but you were just as condescending, treating her vapid nouveau riche adaptation of fashionable Muslim values as if it were sincere. That girl was no virgin. I've seen her at orgies that would make you blush even if you saw them on the screen in the private darkness of an Amsterdam

porno theater. You were her unknowing pimp, intro-
ducing her to other Europeans much less gullible and
earnest than you. You are an idiot to believe that drivel
she fed you. Those people are fools. You're smarter
than them. You ought to know there is a more compe-
tent intelligentsia in this city."

He breaks off and jumps to his feet and drinks his Turkish coffee in one swallow. Then he lays the cup gently
upside down on the dented metal tray and strides away.
In a moment he is gone.

Eventually, the second hand on Ib's watch begins to
move again, and he has the muscle control to turn over
Gamal's Turkish coffee cup. The accidental design of
the muddy grounds is supposed to tell fortunes, although he has never before had the slightest curiosity
about this form of divination. Ib sees a side view of a
man holding a mask to his face, except the face behind
the mask is hideously unformed. He closes his eyes for
a moment, then looks more closely. He can no longer
detect any image in the coffee grounds.

Who is this man Gamal? The California accent means he
might be upper class, educated at some time or another

39

in the States. He could be the son of a diplomat or a wealthy businessman. The latter is more likely, because diplomats are usually stationed in Washington or New York. But it is possible he is the bright child of the lower middle class who won a scholarship to an American university, or a former émigré who drove a limousine or built architectural models for a few years in Los Angeles until he had enough money to return home and marry his childhood sweetheart. "All this," Ib says, laughing out loud and poking his food, "because he spoke one sentence of English with an accent that may have been from California." A man at the next table turns to look, just as Ib is poised to project a bean into his mouth. Ramadan. The cannon has not sounded yet. The men at this teahouse are still fasting. Ib places the guilty bean back on its battered aluminum plate. Across the street on a three-legged stand is a globe-shaped brass kettle for cooking beans and rice. Half a dozen men huddle around the kettle, each fondling a plastic package containing red liquid and strips of eerily white pickled radishes.

"The guy who just left," Ib says in Arabic to the man nearest him, "where was he from?" The neighbor shakes his head. "Have you ever seen him before?" No, again. "Why was he so funny?" The man ponders this question for a moment. His answer makes him excited as he tells it. Gamal did an imitation of a famous actor who was in a government television commercial for birth control. In fact, Ib's neighbor seems to think he *was* this actor. He consults his friends. They discuss the possibility. Some dismiss the idea out of hand. A famous actor would never visit this district, not even during Ramadan. Many rich Egyptians do slum around Husseyn Square, but that is several miles away. Other nearby café patrons join in to weigh the possibility that this actor has been in their midst. Ib listens, fascinated, baffled, unable to translate after a time. The thin film of isolation floats over him again.

Ib reminds himself that he does not care if he offends these Muslims. He drinks his coffee very slowly and stares at each bean for a long while before squeezing the meat out of its skin into his mouth. No one pays any attention.

Ib followed an elaborate maze of movements today before and after meeting the first Gamal in Zamalek along

41

the Nile. It is clear that the two Gamals are one and the same man, and Ib is impressed. His movements after Gamal Number One were irrational, spur-of-the-moment. His behavior must have looked very much as if he were trying to shake an undercover policeman. Ib took a taxi to one place, one personal landmark, only to decide on arrival to jump into a second taxi in the opposite direction to another end of the city. He threw himself into a crowd leaving a huge lecture hall at Cairo University, and then again along the upper-middle-class shopping street, Kasr el Nil; he chased a bus and recklessly jumped onto its rear platform instants before it came to its next stop; he leaped onto a subway train as it was pulling out of the station, not because he had to but because so many other Egyptians did, daring fate, as if conscious of the tragic overcrowding in the country and saying, in effect, "What's one less Egyptian, Allah?" Ib loves the feel of a thousand bodies per one hundred yards in the narrow centuries-old fabric souk, arms bumping elbows.

The cannon booms and all talk stops. The first call to prayer wails nearby, without an amplifier, a beautiful and haunting sound. Other muezzins respond, some with recorded calls, some with scratchy amplifiers, some in their own naked voice, weaving a densely layered tapestry of the common-sense advice that praying is better than not praying. Everyone in the coffeehouse turns away from Ib. He knows this is because they are turning toward Mecca, not bowing but at least making the gesture of turning. But he can't help feeling they are rejecting him. He avoids looking at their shared moment of togetherness, at the whole country's collective prayer. He tries to ignore the crescendo of silverware clinking against plates. Down the street, just at a sharp turn, a man stands alone. The image at first reassures Ib. Here is another person not involved in the massive, communal act of giving thanks, another mere observer like Ib. It is darker now. He cannot see as well through the twilight. He squints. Piece by piece, the visual puzzle of Gamal smoking a cigarette comes together. In the next frame, Ib finds himself striding toward him, calling, "Tell me who you are." As Ib nears him, Gamal calmly stubs the cigarette against the building, flicks the butt into the street, and disappears out of view. Ib breaks into a run and seconds later realizes the waiter from the coffeehouse has also joined the chase. Ib neglected to pay. Without stopping, Ib extracts his wallet,

43

counts two pounds, and throws the notes into the street behind him. The waiter skids to a stop, stumbles, does a rolling fall. Onlookers laugh and clap.

Now that they have shaken the waiter, Ib and Gamal slow to a fast walk. There are still a dozen yards between them. When Ib speeds up, Gamal does too, though he never seems to glance back to see how far behind his pursuer is. If Ib slows, so does Gamal. Gamal has a knack for finding crowds. This is a feat, because nearly everyone has abandoned the streets for leisurely *iftar* dinners. But in the endless old city the two of them come upon one square or length of street after another where people have congregated. When Ramadan falls during the warmer months, families and neighbors gather outdoors. Some eat at enormously long tables and mill around. A quarter mile of curving street, at one point, is filled with such tables, a whole district of people assembled convivially—a charity feast organized by the Muslim Brotherhood. Invitations to join the meal issue from dozens of lips. Gamal shakes hands and laughs and speaks one or two words, but he never stops moving. Ib has more trouble freeing himself, because he does not know the language as well or does not know how rude he's being, and because men stand up to embrace him and pull him into their celebrations, which does not happen to Gamal. But the mysterious figure always remains in Ib's sight. Even when he jumps onto a moving bus, at the front, Gamal seems to have calculated that the bus will slow after a moment to allow a panicked Ib to jump onto the rear well, with four boys cheering and reaching out to help him. When they run out of crowds, Gamal appears to panic and doubles back on his route. Several times the two men nearly collide, and Ib forgets momentarily that he is chasing this man, letting Gamal slip away again, down an alley, into a shop that has a rear exit onto another walkway and nest of shops. They round a corner, one on the heels of the other, and come to a cul-de-sac. Gamal reverses direction, but Ib has him securely by the arm. "Stop," Ib says. "And tell me who the hell you are."

"Look," Gamal says. He is pointing to a window. "We are home," he says. They have inadvertently retraced their steps and are back at Gamal's "apartment." The barber has turned off the one bulb in his shop, so no blue light spills into the street. Gamal puts his arm over Ib's shoulder and walks him past this subtly reconstructed scene. "We will talk, but let's keep moving."

They pass the prayer tents again. The European Sufis have joined the crowd in the other tent. They are all seated, holding plates, eating and talking with vigorous arm movements. Each European is among his own group of Egyptians. The sheikh in the leather jacket sees Ib and waves, inviting them in. Ib is tempted by the seductive smell of curry, and, he must admit, also by the friendliness and the evident integration of these foreigners into the fabric of Egyptian life. But Gamal has Ib firmly by the arm and says, "Please. Don't go in there. I have been rude. I'll act better. I need someone to talk to." Ib frees his arm and thinks it over. The sheikh nods at Ib, as if to say, Go with the Egyptian. Ib is trapped: either decision looks like the will of God or the wish of this sheikh. But Ib has never felt so happily under the spell of chance as he does just now. He goes with Gamal.

▲ ▼ ▲ ▼ ▲ ▼ ▲ ▼ ▲ ▼ ▲

They pass a small grocery store and Ib interrupts Gamal, who is finishing a story. "Just a moment," Ib says. "I have to make a phone call."

Ib enters the tiny store. Boxes of Bioklena soap are stacked to the ceiling. On top of a tall jug of pickled carrots and cauliflowers rests a crate overflowing with small bags of potato chips—a recent American product fattening up Egyptians. Ib's stomach rumbles. No one emerges from the back room to greet him. Voices drift out from an *iftar,* forks and knives clatter, the dissonant sound of family life competes with the harmonious expressions of pleasure at good food, God's gifts, the bounty of Ramadan. Ib fishes a fifty-piastre note from his pocket and lays it gently on the counter next to the phone for the call. He listens to the warm human noise filtering out from within. They are eating pigeon, cooked with garlic and oregano.

He's forgotten whom he needed to call so urgently. He wipes the mouthpiece of the telephone with his handkerchief anyway. He never owned handkerchiefs before he moved to Egypt. He dials the number of his friend Bill. He calls Bill because it is the only number he can remember at this moment. The earpiece crackles deafeningly, so that he must hold the receiver several inches away from his head.

Bill answers. "You have reached the residence of Bill Sarazin. How may I help you?" Ib chuckles at the miniature self-portrait of this greeting: the complete sentences, the readiness to aid a stranger who has not yet identified himself, the stubborn use of English when the majority of the phone calls one receives are wrong numbers, mystified Egyptians who insist on speaking their own tongue. But the phone goes dead before Ib can say hello. He clicks the switch hook several times. He redials Bill's number. Now it is busy. Ib takes two bags of ketchup-flavored potato chips, which cost twenty-five piastres each. He exits the grocery, and Gamal is gone. He devours the chips, even though they taste like dried blood.

Ib drifts over to the stone steps of a mosque and sits down. He is still tipsy from lack of food. He is sorry he misplaced Gamal, but low blood sugar creates its own logic. To suffer the same hunger-induced mania 14 million neighbors enjoy is a curious pleasure. Ib thinks of the Coptic Christians, who try to outfast the Muslims during Ramadan, manufacturing their own holy days and twenty-four-hour fasts. The worn concave step he sits on is level with the street. A small waterless moat lies underneath him and below the road. The base of the moat was the original height of the ground when the mosque was built, but the street has risen four feet in eight hundred years. The moat is a buffer against vehicular traffic, which is now beginning to resume after Ramadan's daily miracle of the half-hour lull around sunset. At no other time of year during waking hours is the city so quiet. The air tastes like a dust storm, but the breeze is cool and clean against Ib's cheek, and the sky is still clear blue, though a darker blue now.

Someone taps Ib lightly on the shoulder. A teenage girl is offering him a glass of water and pulped dates. By sign language she indicates that Ib is welcome to break his fast now. She nods at a shop across the street, where three men wave. Her large green eyes follow Ib's hands, which move slowly to close the pocket-sized notebook he was about to write in. Ib thanks her and accepts the date water. He sips the sweet soothing drink, and the girl says, *"La ilaha illa Allah"* (there is no god but God). Tonight is supposed to be *Laylat al-Qadr,* Night of Worth, when the Qur'an was first revealed to Muhammad, the holiest night of Ramadan. But because the mullahs never know which day Ramadan will end no one can be sure it's *Laylat al-Qadr.*

The girl skips away. On the street she runs into a speeding figure, a man in a hooded cape. Four arms fly out. The girl laughingly rests a hand on her hip as prelude to some more complex teasing gesture, but a single word from the stranger pierces her elegant composure, and she deflates. She walks sadly away. The man in the cape seems to puff up with the girl's lost joy, and he stomps through the mud puddles until he comes to Ib. He throws back the hood theatrically, revealing a nearly bald head rimmed with handsome closely cropped gray hair, like a halo that has slipped. His intense stare pierces Ib, undoing the calm the girl gave him.

Ib imagines the cape is from a play rehearsal, and the stranger is rushing home in costume, late for *iftar.* The cape is tattered in spots, stained, lived-in. Ib has never seen an outfit like this in Cairo, where people take pleasure in imitating each other, where individuality is considered unhealthy. This character may be thirty and prematurely bald and gray or a youthful fifty. Ib doesn't recognize Egyptian or Nubian or Turkish features on his maniacal face, whose outstanding trait is its large nose. It is hard to place his caste. This neighborhood is known for its hashish and heroin business, but unlike an American or European city district where such rough trade occurs, this is a safe place to be—for a foreigner. Cairenes who don't live here stay away with good reason lest the locals suspect they are police informers.

The man in the cape bows on one knee and for an instant Ib recognizes something about the face. He pulls the hood over his head again, and he bursts into a sprint. He is gone.

The abrupt departure triggers the story Gamal was telling when Ib interrupted him to make his phone call. It is as if the story appears on a single sheet of paper in Ib's mind. Ib opens his notebook and quickly writes down what he remembers of Gamal's tale.

Charles Mattimore spends his days this way since he arrived in Egypt for a two-week visit with us two months ago. He rises precisely at ten. Who knows if he actually sleeps or simply sits in his chair by the bed watching the idea of himself asleep. Our maid says his bed is never disturbed by slumber. He uses the bathroom for exactly thirty minutes and does not leave behind a trace of himself. He arrives at the formal dining room table at ten-thirty. The first morning—we had long since breakfasted and scattered—he sat quietly, hands folded in front of him, for some time before Hoda noticed. He delivered his order in that plain clipped Oxford English of his and although Hoda speaks no English (and Charles claims

not a word of Arabic has ever sullied his throat) somehow they worked out his unvarying morning meal:
strong French coffee, American bacon burnt to a crisp,
eggs in a curried cream sauce on toast, and half a melon
sprinkled judiciously with the juice of one lemon. He
leaves the building at eleven, buys the London *Times* at
the Marriott Hotel. He takes a taxi to the American University, which fired him last year. He finds a somewhat
secluded but also visible spot out of the foot traffic in
the main courtyard. He rests his thin Bond Street briefcase on his lap and reads his newspaper and eventually
entertains former students, who gather in twos and
threes around him. He is always home by five o'clock
for cocktails with us on the balcony. He never eats out.
He does have a mysterious source of duty-free wine,
not the sour local wine which is all we can get here.
This is the only reason we did not kick him out weeks
ago. My sister-in-law works in the department that fired
him. She says cryptically that Charles has returned to
Cairo to die. He is thirty-nine years old and seems in
good health, if a bit pale. The University's dean has re-
quested that I ask Charles to spend his days elsewhere.
My wife wonders if we will find him one day with his
brains blown out in the guest room, but otherwise

neatly groomed and ready for cocktails. We cannot figure out how to dislodge him. Perhaps we don't want to.
He can be so charmingly unpleasant that we forget our
own quarrels and feel happy together. My daughter Annahíd is the only one who likes him unreservedly, although I notice she keeps a distance of several feet
between herself and him at all times, a unique precau-
tion in her social behavior.

Ib reads what he has written. The fact that he remembers the tale surprises him; he was not listening carefully when Gamal told it. He likes the way he feels
Gamal's life around its edges. Ib is accustomed to the
happy sensation of losing his sense of self in Cairo, as if
there were no "I," but he has never seen things from an
Egyptian perspective. He did not reveal to Gamal that
he also knows this Charles Mattimore. The portrait is
accurate but also well beyond what Ib knows of
Charles. He slips the notebook into his jacket pocket
and stands up. The sky is completely dark. Bare bulbs
dangle blindingly from the walls of random buildings.
Midget trucks, cars, motorbikes, donkey carts, and hundreds of people swarm in the narrow street. They smell

satisfied. Ib takes a few tentative, dizzy steps. A car blinks its lights at him, not to tell him to move out of the way, but simply to welcome him back to the stream of life.

Ib comes to a large construction site in an irregularly shaped open area formed by the convergence of two main roads. Port Said Street is jammed with foot and motor traffic, a tiny part of the million visitors to nearby Husseyn Square every night of Ramadan. The other feeder street is empty except for two boys playing soccer—the goalie is paralyzed from the waist down. Kleig lights for the construction crew give the feel of a movie set. Wooden fences prevent passersby from seeing what is being built or demolished. Every other public works project is halted during the evening because of Ramadan. This one must be important or financed by the French, who are notorious for ignoring local customs. Port Said Street follows the path of the old Khalij al-Masri canal, hence its riverlike meandering. Ribbons of dust weave in and out of the fierce buzzing lights. A giant hammer behind the fence begins to pound the earth. Each thud resounds under Ib's feet, many dozen yards away. A bus with a handwritten cardboard sign stating its destination is Bawiti creeps by, men hanging out the rear well. A conductor with one filmy gray eye hands a ticket to the man dangling furthest out of the bus, exchanging it for the ten-piastre note with two deft fingers and a thumb. Ib is close enough to ask—and he does ask—the men hanging out the bus if they expect to survive the five-hour trip to the desert oasis town of Bawiti, close enough to sniff the breath of one of these men, which smells like roses. Not one of Ib's ten thousand neighbors appears to pay any heed to the ear-splitting thuds of the hammer. "Bawiti?" the men shout and laugh at Ib. "Wait here," one of them says. "The bus will be back in ten minutes, *insh'allah.*" The last face Ib sees on the bus as it chugs around a bend is that of Gamal, who waves goodbye with only his index finger.

He is not sure if this is the café he was thinking about or if it's another one around the corner. Alerted only by the forest-floor aroma of sandalwood incense, he walks on a few steps as if he were in a hurry. Then he remembers he is in no hurry, has nowhere to go, is out in the city tonight exactly for a turquoise-tiled teahouse like this one. When he sits down he tells the waiter in Arabic that this city makes foreigners feel rushed. The waiter laughs through tanned teeth. He is a large man but holds his galabiya hem between two fingers the way a child holds a security blanket. He shakes a man by the shoulder at a neighboring table of men—the stranger in the cape whom Ib saw earlier. These coincidences do not trouble Ib at all. Cairo is one of the largest cities in the world, but still a small town. The waiter translates what Ib said, even though Ib spoke in Arabic: "Foreigners think they have to run very fast just to stay in one place in Cairo." The caped stranger turns to Ib, who is now sorry he addressed the waiter. You never talk to one Egyptian, you talk to all of them. The man in the cape smiles goofily and says in English, "You are American! Come sit at our table! Have *shisha* pipe!" The water in one of these pipes bubbles seductively somewhere behind Ib, and the sweet brown smell of the smoke wafts over his shoulder.

"Talk Arabic," Ib says. "I am not American. You can see I speak Arabic well." The whole table laughs at this last remark, not necessarily because of Ib's pronunciation, but because Egyptians find *khawagas* speaking Arabic unaccountably amusing. Blood rushes to Ib's face.

The spokesman smiles intelligently now and says, in cultured Arabic, "You *do* speak Arabic, but, sadly, no one speaks Arabic *well* anymore."

Ib embraces this man's thought, and they shake hands vigorously, with all the strength of a blooming friendship. Ib decides he is a journalist, perhaps a theater critic, because they are a few blocks from 26th of July Street and the theater district. Ib is reflecting on the perils of friendship in translation and wondering where he's seen this man before when a set of light feminine hands land on his shoulders.

Ib's friend Lena drifts airily into view. "Here you are," Ib says to her in Dutch. "I waited an hour for you in front of the theater."

Lena studies Ib carefully after this remark. They have made no plans to meet tonight, are not even on very good terms when they do bump into each other lately (Lena thinks Ib treated a Canadian girlfriend of hers badly). But Lena is sharp and she sees that Ib is in some kind of trouble. Ib pays the waiter for the coffee he did not have. Lena asks the bald man at the next table if he minds her taking Ib off their hands. "He escaped from the hospital a few hours ago," she stage-whispers in Arabic. "But we weren't worried. He hasn't strangled anyone for years." Ib laughs at this improvisation, but he also feels a pang nipping in the bud the friendship with this interesting fellow.

"He writes for *Al Ahali*," the leftist newspaper, Ib tells Lena. She takes his hand and puts his arm over her shoulder, tucking herself in close to him. "Or I want him to be the sort of person who writes for *Al Ahali*," he says. She keeps an eye on him, squinting, as they walk the few blocks to her husband's theater. Lena has an Egyptian father and a Dutch mother. She is well read in many of the things Ib studies, a pretty and playful woman, a native of Cairo. He sees her socially. He teases her for talking so fast, for constantly interrupting him. She is a manic woman, operating at a different speed than Ib. But he gets drunk once in a while and flirts with her in English. In Dutch their interactions are asexual, perhaps because she is so smart and no-nonsense in her two native tongues, but she is less confident of English, a little bit languid when she speaks it, and to tell the truth, Ib is intimidated by her in Dutch and in Arabic. Lena flirts back only to annoy her Egyptian husband, a director of plays who has never liked

Ib. Yehya thinks Ib is wasting his talents on this easy expatriate lifestyle.

They step into the darkened lobby of the theater and stomp dirt and straw off their shoes. The aroma of roasted peanuts and burnt-sugar candy brings tears to Ib's eyes and conjures a phantom—his stepfather's narrow canal-front house in Amsterdam, where Ib and his mother lived for a year after the divorce from his father. The house stood next to a small, fastidiously clean adult movie theater that had ruffled curtains in its windows. His sisters had declined to come along to Holland, because of high school boyfriends or college, but at the funeral they said Ib had betrayed their father by going to Amsterdam, the first time he'd ever heard this accusation. None of them had felt any allegiance to their father, who had quickly moved in with a thirty-two-year-old professor of dance. The four sisters stayed at the old house by themselves (Susan went to nearby Smith College), and they had the time of their lives under the unwatchful eye of their father, who paid visits at exactly the same hour and on the same day each week. But Ib is not remembering his stepfather; he is revisiting the cinema next door that gave him his education in sex. Lena notes his tears.

She asks if he is drunk, then she zooms in close as if about to kiss him, but she is merely smelling his breath. Ib shakes his head. "But that's a good idea," he says. They walk arm-in-arm again into the auditorium, his hand creeping up her ribs. Yehya is running his actors through their paces, without words, to get the movements down. He speaks their cues, fragments of theater talk, and the actors shuffle gloomily here and there, standing up, sitting down, tangling and untangling bodies, lying on the floor. The play is an American farce, full of physical comedy. The slapstick is barely discernible in the deliberate movements on stage.

Yehya senses someone in the back of the theater and stands up, peering into the lights with cupped hands as if through binoculars. Ib waves, then pulls Lena in front of him, momentarily palming a breast, and gives her a passionate stage kiss. Yehya's laughter echoes in the auditorium.

Lena jerks away from Ib, who is equally surprised by the kiss. They both say, at the same instant, "Sorry." They sit in the last row of seats. Ib stares at his fingernails for a while.

Finally, Lena says, "Yehya and I are trying to have a baby." She goes red, runs her hand through her hair. Ib has a brief image of her lying on her back naked in bed, after *he's* made love to her slowly and carefully, her knees now hugging her chest to keep his sperm inside her. He is surprised by the intricacy of these fantasies. He glances over at the furrowed brow on her beautiful face and wonders if perhaps she is thinking this way, too.

But she says, "Yehya won't go to a doctor. He's not being overmasculine about it. Doctors terrify him." Ib suggests that she secretly take a cup of— "No!" Lena says, laughing, but then: "It's a good idea. I could collect it—" She stops. She looks Ib square in the eye, catching him chewing a thumbnail. It feels for a moment as if she were sizing him up.

"Yehya is having more trouble with the censors over his movie," she says, apparently to change the subject. "They insist he either eliminate every shot of the German woman's breasts or airbrush each frame so that no nipples show. He says this is a triumph, even though he fights with them every day. He wants to make them think

61

they are doing damage to the integrity of the film so they won't wake up and realize they would normally stop production because of its openly sexual situations. Of course, it will be banned in the end, but maybe he can finish it and slip it out of the country to a film festival."

Ib says, "So how else can we talk about sex without . . ." He does not finish his thought: without having it. Even half-expressed, the romantic delusion makes him feel boyish and stupid. He steals a peek at Lena, who is smiling awkwardly at him. Ib looks away, feeling warmth spread from his nipples down his ribs.

"Oh God, how stupid of me to talk only of our problems," she says. "You must feel terrible. I heard all about your Egyptian girlfriend." Ib asks what girlfriend. "You were going to be married, ya?" She puts her head in her hands. "I'm so silly," she whispers. "You must think I'm such a—how do they say in American—a nerd?" Her assertion sinks in, but the sweet musky smell of her exposed Dutch underarm hair drifting up at him confuses the urge Ib has to deny the basic facts of this rumor. Now he desperately wants to take Lena in his hands and lick her whole body and enter her by tiny increments.

Finally, he asks, "Are you talking about the woman at the National Library?" Lena nods. "We were not going to marry. That's ridiculous. It just another story circulating in this city of bad translations. I never touched her."

Lena sits up and looks at him and arches her back as if it aches—a signal of her annoyance with him perhaps, but the gesture also reveals her lovely figure.

"The moment I start talking about this woman . . . ," he says. "I don't know if I can explain. I know I'm telling the truth but it sounds—even to me—as if I'm lying. It's like the summer I spent in Crete with two friends and their two young children. For the whole summer the village could not decide who was the father, me or him. Then he went off to Morocco for a month and I became substitute Baba. And I would meet beautiful single women on the beach and try to explain to them that the child I was carrying home asleep in my arms was *not* my son or daughter, and even I thought I was telling the most pathetic lie. The women always looked at me with such sad tenderness: this poor unhappily married father. There is no story about this Egyptian woman at the National Library. I know nothing about her. She just took a few days off from the library last week."

"No, no," Lena says. "I have heard the story in many places. You are in love. She is a short story writer, she writes for *Rose al-Yusef*. Her family is Christian, but they do not accept you."

Flustered, but also amused, Ib says, "Lena. Look at me sitting here with you. I know the story of my own life. I have never spoken a single word of consequence to this woman."

"But a very good friend of mine knows her. Charles. You don't know him. He does not make things up. He is very literal-minded. Believe me, this story is true about some-one, maybe not you, but it has attached itself to you like an eel. You had better have it removed. My husband has heard it several times, too, among our Egyptian friends, in Arabic. It's not just one of these expatriate stories."

Ib says, "Charles Mattimore? Charles is a born liar and the least literal-minded man I know. He loves telling stories simply to disconcert people."

They are silent for a moment. Yehya turns to observe where Lena and Ib ought to be every so often, but he can't see them because he's dimmed the house lights

and turned up the stage lights. The actors on stage go
through their paces quietly, intent on getting the right
nuances, doing the physical comedy in painstakingly
slow motion over and over again. Yehya's instructions to
the actors are clever and easy to visualize. Ib has never
before so clearly understood Yehya's talent as a director.

Someone else walks down the aisle, and Yehya turns to
scan him. The dark figure wears a baseball cap and
walks slowly to emphasize each creak in the wooden
floor planks of the aisle. He stage-whispers in a Clint
Eastwood voice, "Hey, Yah-Heeyah, don't ya know it's
Ramadan. These kids here are supposed to be home
with their mamas and daddies." Yehya claps for his actors' attention. "Let's take five," he says in English. "We
have a special guest I've asked to talk to you. He has
written a brilliant play that no one will produce because . . . shall we say, it is subversive of the present order of things. It is about a group of Muslim immigrants
to North America in the 1850s who try to set up an in-
dependent country in Nevada. Our guest is going to
talk to you about American mannerisms, body language, and social behavior. We are honored to have
with us," and then Yehya pronounces a name that
sounds like "Gamaliyya," the part of the old city where

Ib has spent most of his evening, but not a man's name that Ib has ever heard before. The stranger in the baseball cap climbs up on stage, still Clint Eastwood. When he throws his hat into the theater, he sheds his character. At first, he does not show his face to the mostly empty seats of the theater, because the actors on stage are his audience. But something about his body language is familiar to Ib.

He whispers to Lena, "Isn't that the theater critic I met at the café? Wait—I know him. It's Gamal. This guy has been following me around the city all day. He works for the Ministry of the Interior."

She laughs. *"Allemaal onzin,"* she says in Dutch. "Nonsense. He's one of our best friends. We had coffee with him at the Gezirah Club this morning. He's Armenian but he grew up in Cairo." She pauses. "You met him this morning after your tennis game," she says in English. "But, oh, that's right. He was wearing some silly wig for a play he's doing. We introduced you to him, but we probably forgot to explain that he is wearing a wig. The problem with Gamal-Leon is that he loves to play a practice joke—what is the phrase? Practical joke, ya. You learn to ignore the joke, to act as if nothing were wrong." She has returned to Dutch. "He really can be a pest. He's actually Yehya's friend. I don't know if I like him all that much, or if I understand him. To tell the truth, he disturbs me sometimes. I think he is a very troubled man."

▲ ▼ ▲ ▼ ▲ ▼ ▲ ▼ ▲ ▼ ▲

They are in a taxi zooming down the exit ramp off the October 6 Bridge to visit Gamal's in-laws. Gamal speaks to the driver and they are now turning wildly onto *Shari' Gezirah*. Christmas lights strung up in trees beside an open-air restaurant create the momentary sensation of being on a roller coaster. The taxi stops a few doors from the building where Ib lives. He says nothing to Gamal of this. They have pulled up so close to a donkey cart full of trash that both Gamal and Ib will have to exit the car on the driver's side. Gamal hands the driver fifty piastres, half as much as Ib would have given. The driver will not take the five bills. Gamal says to Ib in English, "You're the reason he charges extortion rates for such a dangerous trip. He thinks he can raise the price because he raised our pulses, isn't that so, *ya rais?*" he asks the driver. "He is quite mistaken." Gamal makes a show of removing ten piastres from the total.

67

Very delicately he scrapes the remaining bills across the taxi driver's stubbled chin. The intimacy of this gesture shocks Ib. They all sit quietly for a time. Finally, the driver sighs, accepts the money, and Gamal and Ib climb out of the cab.

Dust swirls around them. The odor from the donkey cart is appalling—rotten grapefruit, human urine, animal shit, and coffee—but after one adjusts to it, the scent becomes pleasant. The Nile lies twenty feet below them. A riverbus thunders by, its unmuffled engine shaking the leaves of the palm trees above. Fishermen hop back and forth between two rowboats tied up to an abandoned floating restaurant. Two adults and six children sleep on the two boats.

"Ib," Gamal says. "What sort of name is Ib? What does it mean, other than the chief djinn Iblis? I believe you made up the name because of the crisis this poor wronged girl has plunged you into. I don't think you even remember your own name or national identity. Am I right?"

Ib laughs. "For the last time. That story is untrue. She may have been sick with the flu for a few days. She

68

might have taken a vacation." Gamal nods distractedly, not listening.

He leads Ib by the arm across the street. The building they enter has a gold plaque on the wrought iron door of the elevator, the type of exposed-cage elevator that unnerves Ib. The plaque says, *H. Kimball Johnson & Stephen Faulk, American Oil Exploration.* But a woman's voice from the street calls, "*Ya* Gamal, Gamal-Leon." They return outdoors.

She has liquid oval Egyptian eyes, but sandy blond hair. Over her hair she wears a scarf, which reveals more than it conceals. Her long blue dress falls to her ankles, but her figure is plain to see: big hips, handsome breasts, long legs, full fleshy arms. In the States, the women Ib fell in love with were skinny and small-breasted, like Lena. Egypt has broadened his tastes. The woman who called Gamal stands in the street, waiting for a cab. She and Gamal speak softly and rapidly in Arabic, mixed with French. Ib has lagged behind and when he approaches them Ib sees her face more clearly. Talking with Gamal caused her to frown. Ib's presence brings an attractive smile to what Ib realizes is a beautiful face. She switches to English, with a nod to

Ib, although she is still speaking privately with Gamal.

"Do you want a key or not? I have the extra," she says. Gamal's back is to Ib. He grunts no. One of his hands rests lightly on an American four-wheel-drive vehicle, the index finger tapping the glossy red paint. "Do stop that," she says, of his tapping. He stops, and her raised eyebrow indicates she is both surprised and grateful that he obeyed her wish. "Well, have it your way. I am in a hurry. Doris is going to drive me to the hospital in Ma'adi. We're meeting at her sister's house." She turns to Ib and, although she is crying, extends a hand to him as if unacknowledged tears rolling down her cheeks were an ordinary event. Ib shakes her hand. "I am Safeyya. I think we've met somewhere. At Andrew Shoukri's perhaps? No, the Dutch Institute. You gave a very intelligent talk on Rumi. Your translations were lovely. I am sorry to hear of your father's death. Forgive me for running off and not asking you upstairs to talk about your work, Ib."

Such personal knowledge of him, and the casual mention of it, startles Ib. He has never met this woman before—he's sure he would remember her—yet she knows intimate details of his recent history, even if she has them a little wrong.

At that moment, the same taxi Ib and Gamal rode in turns onto *Shari' Gezirah,* and Safeyya puts one finger in the air. The Peugeot glides to a stop in front of her. She slips gracefully into the car, and it speeds off. She leaves behind the low-tide fragrance of ambergris.

They reenter the building, and Ib says, "She is lovely, but she made me feel—I don't know . . ." "Like a child?" Gamal says. "No, no," Ib says. "She made me feel important, likable. This is a gift some women have—and no man I've ever met." Ib thinks about what he's just said. "That sounds pretty stupid. I don't know what I'm saying. Is she your wife?"

A rattle comes from deep in Gamal's throat, something like a laugh. "Would that I were so lucky," he says. He presses the call button for the elevator. "She's my sister-in-law. We don't get along. I won't explain. Arab men do not enjoy indulging strangers in family gossip. If I were Arab, you would not have seen her." He's right. The Egyptian men Ib knows who have not lived abroad

71

do not talk of, let alone introduce, their wives to strangers. Nevertheless, Ib asks if she is married. In his three years in Egypt Ib has never asked this question about an Egyptian woman. Gamal says, "Yes. Come, let's take the stairs." The elevator arrives just as Gamal bounds onto the first landing. Ib rebels and steps into the brass cage.

"Which floor?" Ib calls. Gamal holds up five fingers. The elevator is slow. They arrive at the fifth floor at the same time. A big receptionist's desk sits empty. Gamal bolts into the office area. Ib follows but loses him. The sound of another man's helpless American laughter leads Ib to Gamal in a spacious office. Every piece of furniture has to have been imported from the States. A barrel-chested mid-fortyish American man stands up behind his black teak desk, and he thrusts out a huge sunburned hand. His grip is a friendly but convincing display of American strength. In his presence Ib feels slightly less American than he felt the moment before meeting him.

"Pleasure to make your acquaintance," the American says. "Very fond of this fellow here. He is the only Egyptian I know who can throw a curveball. The name is Kimball Johnson, but call me Jack." Ib says he would prefer to call him Mr. Johnson, a momentary lapse into honesty—the man is so big. Both Jack and Gamal find this hilarious. Ib examines the room and Gamal in the room carefully while their laughter burps and dwindles. Despite what Kimball Johnson said, Ib gets the feeling this man and Gamal are essentially strangers. But Gamal seems at home here. Ib realizes Gamal-Leon has inhabited every space they've passed through this evening as if it were home, which is an ability Ib admires. Even this masculine, sterile, cigar- and fart-scented sanctuary of Americanness is home.

Kimball Johnson says, "Gamal tells me you want me to give some sort of character reference for him?" Ib must look puzzled, for he is. Johnson reacts quickly. "Well damn it, Gamal. You went and pulled my leg again and I declared that was the last time yesterday, four-fifteen in the afternoon, if you recall. Even wrote it down on the hospital wall."

Gamal nods, but does not look particularly interested in what Kimball Johnson is saying. His chair is tipped back. His feet are jammed against Johnson's expensive desk.

Gamal points at Ib and says, "This is a shadow of a man. His stepfather died the other day. He had a fight with his sisters because he inherited money from the stepfather and they didn't. He hasn't slept with a woman in over a year. He lives in Egypt, but he doesn't know why. My question, Jack, is what would you do for a fellow like this back in Texas? Take him to a cathouse in the meatpacking district? Push him from a Lear jet at ten thousand feet? Set him up in business for himself selling mineral rights out from under the feet from poor dumb Okies?"

Kimball Johnson has been pouring bourbon for his guests. He hands a glass to Ib and says, "From my experience with this man, which is all of about thirty-six hours now, I'd say the best thing to do is let a speech like that hang on the vine for a while. Then you just flick it with one finger and it drops to the ground." He gives Gamal his shot glass, and Gamal pours the drink into the dirt of a woolly cactus plant on Kimball Johnson's desk. Johnson sighs and sits back in his chair.

Gamal says, "Here's a joke. Anwar el-Sadat sees an American oil geologist making his one allotted phone call from Hell. When he's done, the American has to pay

one million dollars for a five-minute call. Sadat is
shocked and terrified. 'Well, I'll just talk for a few seconds,' he says to himself. 'I can't afford much of anything these days.' But Sadat, being Egyptian, of course
gets carried away and talks for half an hour. When he
hangs up he asks, fearfully, how much he owes.
'Twenty-five piastres,' the clerk says. 'For half an hour!
Why so little?' Sadat asks. 'It's a local call,' the clerk says."

Kimball Johnson laughs, but softly. Ib has heard the
joke before, so he does not find the punch line as
amusing as he once did, although he remembers with
regret being convulsed with laughter over the joke. But
Johnson, after just a moment's pleasure, looks stricken.

"This," he says, "is the sign of a very unhappy country,
my friend. We tell jokes like that in Texas but they are
unfortunately about Negroes or Mexicans. You should
not be telling these stories about yourselves. I believe it
is unhealthy."

Gamal stands up and shakes Kimball Johnson's hand.
Gamal nods at Ib to join him on his way out of the office. Ib wonders what Gamal is *not* saying in response
to this remark. Johnson accepts their abrupt departure

without a word. Ib glances at the Texan as they are leaving, and Johnson waves, a girlish little flap of that big hand while he's puffing on a huge cigar in the other.

Gamal says, "I'm going to climb out on the balcony of Johnson's partner's office and break into my flat. I don't have a key. I won't drag you along on this caper. You have graciously suspended your disbelief long enough tonight. You go downstairs and over to the next building and come up to flat fifty. I'll let you in."

Ib says, "Safeyya offered you a key," but Gamal puts a finger to his lips, then hums a few bars from the theme song of the television show "Mission Impossible."

A few moments later, Gamal opens the door for Ib. Inside his dark apartment, he does not turn on any lights but goes directly to a large bookshelf and pulls down a book. He steps over to the French windows, where orange and purple sky provide minimal reading light. He reads: "Ib. Danish: relatively common name, attested since the Middle Ages, probably a vernacular development of Jacob." He flips through more pages. "Aha," he says. "Jacob was the cunning younger twin, who persuaded his fractionally older brother Esau to part with his right to inheritance, in exchange for a bowl of soup. Later he tricked his blind and dying father into blessing him in place of Esau. The derivation of the name has been much discussed. It is traditionally explained as being derived from the Hebrew *akev* ('heel') and to have meant 'heel-grabber,' because when Jacob was born he took hold of Esau's heel."

"And where does Gamal-Leon come from?" Ib asks.

"A tree. A mistake. A lack of any knowledge of English and the word 'chameleon.' My parents thought they were doing me a favor by naming me after Nasser, and after Léon Blum, a hero of my father's. They had no idea combining the names would mark me for life as a quick-change artist, a slippery-tongued mimic who does not know his own voice or face."

Gamal puts the book back on the shelf. He beckons Ib to the balcony from which he made his entrance.

They look out over the city, lovely as it only is at night, especially during Ramadan, when all the colored lights are strung over the minarets and rooftops. Muezzins chant lines of the Qur'an. Women ululate, a high-

77

pitched warbling call of kinship. A couple of buildings down is the rooftop playground of the British School, with emerald green astroturf, volleyball nets, a miniature soccer pitch, and high fences. In the middle of it all a lonely Union Jack flaps in the breeze. Gamal says, "On a rare clear day, you can see the Pyramids from here, rising magnificently over the urban chaos and sadness." Ib has the same view. He reminds Gamal they are going to visit his wife's parents.

Ib asks, "Is Safeyya your wife?" Gamal grimaces, nods. They leave the flat.

Gamal does not speak during the short walk to the building where his in-laws live. His silence is like that of a child kept up past his bedtime. He stifles yawns. His eyes bulge, wide open. Even when they arrive at the lobby of George and Hanaa's building, which is right next door to Ib's, Gamal remains quiet. In the elevator, the blind boy who operates the cage asks Gamal for another English word. Gamal, pretending to be blind himself, pats the boy on his head. "Two words. Prisoner of childhood. Well, that's three words." The boy repeats the words with great seriousness. Gamal supplies the Arabic translation. They arrive at the

twenty-third floor, and the boy feels the elevator to a
stop with his foot. On the twenty-third floor, there is
only one door. A sixty-year-old man answers. This is
Gamal's father-in-law. Ib has seen his intelligent and
sympathetic face in many newspaper photographs. He
is an important government figure, but likable, as few
of those faces in the newspapers are. Ib introduces
himself, briefly describing his adventures with Gamal.
The three of them go to the balcony, where a stunning
fiftyish woman is sitting. The balcony is as understated
and elegant as any Egyptian living space Ib has ever
seen. Two Chinese lanterns and a wealth of softly lit
palm trees—illuminated from inside their pots—provide
a warm glow. A large bottle of Napoleon brandy and a
bowl of fresh figs sit on the table by this woman,
Hanaa. Two glasses have been poured, two others are
awaiting the wayward sons. "In Egypt, one should always be prepared for guests," George says. Gamal-Leon
is led like a sleepwalker to his seat, given a tumbler of
brandy and a cigar, which he cuts and lights. He says
nothing, his face a calm and friendly blank.

The three others speak about him as if he were not
there, commenting on his boundless energy and ability
to mimic anyone within moments of meeting them. Ib

has known Gamal only a few hours but finds he has more stories to tell about him than he has about anyone else he knows in Egypt. Hanaa and George put him completely at ease. They ask Ib about himself, and he summarizes his life story better than he ever has before. George and Hanaa offer insights into his personality and work that he likes enormously, especially the idea that he is more at home here and in his research on Egypt than he realizes. They suggest new directions he might take that are beautifully logical and born of the route he has already traveled. Soon, the three are laughing and finishing each other's sentences like old friends. Hanaa was a dancer in her youth (Ib guesses). Unlike her daughter, she is slim and agile, and Ib enjoys making her laugh, a simple three-step melody, and George seems to encourage the mild flirtation with his wife because it makes her that much more handsome to watch, and both men bask in the reflected light.

The phone rings and Hanaa says, "This will be Safeyya." Husband and wife rise at the same instant and leave Ib to his silent friend. Ib hears them speaking quietly with their daughter, each on separate phones. He watches Gamal for a reaction. None registers. They are high above 26th of July Street, facing north. The flyover that crosses the island hums with traffic, the honking horns pleasantly far away. The air is cool. Ib has not been drinking his brandy, a French import that only Egyptian diplomats or foreigners with press passes can buy in the country. He raises the glass to his nose and inhales, periodically. The city's lights seem to swell and brighten every time he breathes in the brandy. This could be the effect of power surges, but Ib prefers a more romantic explanation.

"Are you going to drink that?" Gamal says. He stands and stubs out what is left of his cigar. "Drink up," he says. "Hurry. Before they get off the phone."

Ib wants to protest. He does not want to leave. He has never liked anyone so quickly and totally as George and Hanaa. He feels at home here, feels as if, by merely asking, he could move in with these people and become part of the family. They relieve something that has been nagging him for some time.

But Gamal is the key to this world. Ib drinks the brandy in one burning gulp and puts down his unlit cigar. Leaving, they pass Hanaa in George's leather-bound study, and Ib taps her shoulder. He is embarrassed to feel her bra strap through the thin silky fabric. She puts

81

the phone to her breast. Ib whispers, "I will bring him home. I'll make sure he gets into no more trouble. You have my word." Hanaa's delighted smile fills Ib with well-being. They close the door just as Hanaa is saying goodbye to Safeyya.

▲ ▼ ▲ ▼ ▲ ▼ ▲ ▼ ▲ ▼ ▲

Ib waits at the coffeehouse in Giza where his new friend has left him. Gamal said he was going to talk to the sister of an old girlfriend who lived nearby about possibly having an affair with Ib tonight. Ib feels silly, certain this is another misconstruction or practical joke, but he also holds out wistful hope that what Gamal promised he will actually do.

Gap-toothed men stand behind the chest-high rectangular counter space in the café. One man, Abdul Messih, which means "the servant of the Messiah" (and is therefore a Christian name), operates the coffee-making apparatus. Abdul Messih is responsible for a metal box full of fine sand that sits on the gas flame. The sand is hot enough to boil liquid and Abdul Messih lets the small brass pot boil over every time into the sand, so that the pungent aroma of burnt coffee and sugar pervades this alley. Fresh laundry hangs from balconies above the coffeehouse. Wet clothes hung during the day bleach and fade, quickly wearing out in the merciless Egyptian sun, so most women—and Ib—hang their laundry at night. The clothes are always dry by morning. But drops of gray liquid fall onto the café's patrons. They feel a splash on their bald pates or forearms and wipe off the droplet, but do not move or even look up for the source of this irritation. Ib's table is the target of three separate drips. Abdul Messih arrives with his coffee and places it directly in the line of one persistent drip. Ib immediately shifts the tray a fraction of an inch, just as the droplet lands, blessedly missing the tiny glass. Abdul Messih can't help noticing this defensive strategy. He laughs and wipes the sweat from his forehead and dries his hands on his filthy apron. He sits down with Ib.

Abdul Messih stares up at the gently fluttering layers of laundry. "My wife gives me the first son this morning," he says in English. "Four daughters and now a son. I am okay." A tear rolls from his eye, which he dabs with the corner of his apron.

Ib says, "I speak Arabic," lightly touching Abdul Messih's arm. The Copt shifts into Arabic without expressing astonishment that Ib speaks it, which endears him to Ib. He tells Ib that he loves his four daughters as much as he loves life. "You must meet them. One day you can marry the one you choose."

Abdul Messih sighs and distractedly shifts Ib's glass of coffee a bit, as it happens back into the range of the laundry drippings. A big drop splashes in the glass. Ib pretends not to notice. He is pondering this strange remark, "Marry the one you choose." No Egyptian, not even a Copt, would offer his daughter's hand to a stranger, let alone a foreigner. Ib decides to test his comprehension of Abdul Messih's generosity. "I will marry the youngest when she is thirteen," Ib says.

"Alhumdulillah," Abdul Messih says, which means "Thanks be to God," not what Ib's remark required: *Insh'allah,* "God willing." Another man behind the counter calls Abdul Messih. "Of course," he says, as he rises to go. "We can't afford two children, never mind five. But since we can't afford two why not have as many as possible!"

Abdul Messih shakes Ib's hand warmly. He turns to go and calls over his shoulder. "Four beautiful daughters and now a son!"

Ib goes next door to a shawerma stand. On the upright spit should be lamb, but this is probably mutton, very fatty, very tasty nevertheless. At this time of night during Ramadan people eat constantly, compulsively. The average Egyptian actually gains weight by the end of Ramadan. A great crowd surrounds the stand, pushing and shoving, but laughing and kidding each other, too. Ib pulls his Massachusetts driver's license from his wallet and waves it in the air. He shouts in English, "I am American. Busy, busy, busy." The crowd parts for him and somehow pulls him to the center. The imperturbable worker slices off piece after piece of the meat, ignoring the clamor around him. Then he carefully scrapes into neat piles the fallen meat and the fried and charred strips of red and green peppers. All during this industrious labor his ten-year-old son has been cutting and opening and splashing with creamy tahini sauce the small pocket breads the delicacies will eventually go in. Finally, to the roaring appreciation of his customers, the father begins to fill the huge pile of prepared pitas.

Without looking at his audience, but somehow knowing what each wants, he passes one, two, three pitas piled precariously on tiny brown cardboard "plates," square but with edges curled up, soon so soggy from sesame oil they are useless as plates. But the meal is delightful. Ib hands the son fifty piastres and eats his shawerma right there, in the middle of the melee.

Gamal seems to have been watching most of this spectacle. He is standing beside a short round woman who wears a full *hegab*, the Muslim scarf over all of her hair (unlike Safeyya, whose scarf was merely ornamental). When Ib reaches them, Gamal says to her in Arabic that Ib is always on duty, so to speak, studying the way crowds move in Cairo. To Ib he says in English, "She speaks only Arabic, one of those rare pure Egyptians. I know she may not seem like much to look at now, but give her time. She has something I consider much more important, a beauty that grows every time you meet her, the ability to surprise you with her soul and presence. I will translate while you have sex with her. What Flaubert calls lovemaking by interpreter."

Ib stares at Gamal, whose eyes dance joyously for the moment. Ib considers leaving here and now, without another word. He's had enough of this fellow. These jokes are not funny and they are not in any way enlightening or useful. "I think I will go home now," he says. He turns, to avoid Gamal, and introduces himself to the woman, in Arabic. She replies, in very good English, that her name is Nur, which she says means "light." Ib's gaze moves slowly back to Gamal-Leon. "You ass," Ib says. Gamal's face collapses. "Wait, wait," Gamal says.

Nur says, "He is not responsible for his acting today. You do not know his story. Difficult and insulting as he is, we must work around him. Perhaps you will reconsider, Mr. Ib, and take him somewhere peaceful and talk with him? I do not think I can experience pleasure in your company tonight, Gamal. Do you understand? Another night, *insh'allah,* you will be more like your old self, which isn't always so easy to take, either." She giggles.

Gamal's shoulders slope forward. He bows his head.

Ib holds the car door for Nur and says goodbye to her, amazed that yet another stranger this evening has imprinted her personality on him in a matter of moments.

▲ ▼ ▲ ▼ ▲ ▼ ▲ ▼ ▲ ▼ ▲

They stumble out of their taxi into the Gezirah Club. Outside this old British bastion of colonial privilege it appears to be snowing in technicolor orange. The *bawabs* stand in their doorways, faces wrapped in scarves, eyes glistening with tears at the dust blown about the wide street. The sky overhead is peach-colored, but khaki toward Roda Island. To walk in this dust storm, a *hamsiin,* is to taste the sky, a grit so fine it does not grate in one's teeth but savors of earth, clay, the mist as it rises from the ancient dirt of Egyptian farms in early morning. But inside the Gezirah Club they seem to have stepped under a glass bubble. The air is clear. The visibility is endless. They can see the dim outlines of the horsetrack and stadium that mark the outer boundary of the club's extensive grounds. Gamal is amazed at this transition, and he remarks excitedly on it to several unimpressed tuxedo-clad Egyptians playing croquet on a grass pitch. One member nods at a nearby guard. The next moment Ib and Gamal are being asked to show their membership cards. "Postcolonialism," Gamal says, laughing bitterly. The security guard holds the two laminated IDs up against a streetlight's brilliant glare. "Let's go to the Marriott Hotel instead," Ib says. Outside, the dust storm howls and whistles. They can plainly see, down the long boulevard packed with double-parked Mercedes inside the Club, that this oasis of reason and clear-thinking is still unperturbed by the *hamsiin* winds.

▲ ▼ ▲ ▼ ▲ ▼ ▲ ▼ ▲ ▼ ▲

The dust storm has ended abruptly, and Ib and Gamal are sitting at a wicker table on the Marriott Hotel grounds under gently swaying palm trees not native to Egypt. It is an interior world, cut off from Cairo by buildings on all sides, and by high fences, gates, and hedges. It is clean, lush, manicured, and reminds Ib of Florida. The green light of the pool behind them flickers against the upper story of the original structure, once a palace. It was the pathetic gift of Ismail to Napoleon III's wife, Empress Eugénie, whom the khedive Isma'il adored more than Egypt, but who, like Egypt, never loved him back. Gamal sips from a tall glass of Stella beer. Ib continues gradually to increase his heart rate with another cup of Turkish coffee.

Two Saudi men come near. One wears a white gown with red headdress and penny loafers. The other wears a black suit with white socks and poufed coiffed hair.

The material of the suit is shiny, scaly, sharkskin or houndstooth. The man in the suit walks like a penguin, perhaps because his shoes are too small. The shoes are patent leather slip-ons that would look more at home on a pretty young Frenchwoman.

A handsome Egyptian woman with hennaed hair stops in front of Gamal and Ib's table, but her back is to them. She begins speaking with these Saudis, the low choked noise of Arabic beautiful in her cadences. Ib cannot decipher their talk, but he watches the woman with care. She wears blue jeans and a black denim jacket whose collar is turned up. Her nails are painted orange and red. She is tall, nearly six feet, towering over the Saudis. She is not deferential but appears to enjoy arguing with them. Despite her Western attire, she is modestly dressed—the jeans are loose-fitting, her black pumps sensible, and her jacket much larger than it needs to be. Only her hair is alluring—luxurious, sparkling, full and softly flowing over her shoulders.

Once, she turns to look at Gamal, then Ib. Her glance is not shy. This woman and her Saudi pals are starting to irritate Ib. They are still standing in front of the table, only a foot away, an acceptable distance for Arabs and

Egyptians, but Ib clenches his teeth. There are plenty of empty tables nearby.

Ib picks up the black notebook he took out of his jacket pocket when they sat down and rises from his chair to take his coffee to another table. "What's in the book?" Gamal asks.

Ib holds up the notebook like a novel he's just decided he no longer wishes to read. He opens it and glances at the story Gamal told him earlier in the evening. Gamal says, "Read something to me. Read to me in that lovely accent of yours." Ib thinks this is a perfect opportunity to play Gamal's own game on him. He reads Gamal's story about Charles Mattimore.

When Ib is finished, Gamal looks up at him with surprisingly friendly green eyes. "Forgive me, I have misread you," he says.

Ib nods, cautiously.

"You know, I had already forgotten it. But you have taken my rough piece of thoughtless tale and turned it into a beautiful woman-shaped story. It is like a vivid dream or a brilliant conversation in a language you don't know well. I am very impressed. I am grateful. In a moment, I'll tell you another story. When Ruqayyah has dismissed these silly Saudis."

The Egyptian woman says to her Saudis, "Enough, *bess*," speaking both the Arabic and English words, and they walk off chastened. She pulls out a chair beside Ib and sits down and confidently smiles at her new neighbor, saying, "I am Ruqayyah." She looks very young, twenty or twenty-one.

Ib asks, "How old *are* you?" The emphasis of the question, as if he'd been speaking with her for some time, flusters him. Sweat leaks from his armpits. His ears burn.

She answers matter-of-factly. "I am twenty-six." She turns to Gamal, all business. "I have spoken with the authorities. A driver will take you to the prison. The government say they have nothing to hide. But they do not apologize for keeping you waiting. You realize that you are being used. Your status as an outsider, *yani*, a member of a very small minority, as well as a Christian, is the only reason you've been called on to do this interview. You

are expected to interview the prisoner, but you are also
expected to twist his words and make him look ridiculous. We will not hold this against you. I am surprised
they chose you. I am not surprised you accepted this as-
signment. You can't resist this strange stage. Meet your
driver in front of the hotel at midnight. He'll recognize
you. Your friend is welcome to join you if he wishes."
She places a hand on Gamal's shoulder and says, "I was
very sorry to hear of little Annahíd's accident. *Alhum-
dulillab,* know that she is in God's embrace." Gamal
grips the arms of his chair as if he were about to fall out
of it. Ruqayyah says. "Ib, I am very rude not to stay and
talk with you. *Insh'allah,* we'll meet again and talk about
Detroit, the center of Islam in America. Do you know
that Islam is the fastest growing religion in the United
States? Your own *Harper's* magazine says so."

With that, she rises and shakes hands with Ib, who does
not even bother to ask her how she knows his name.
Gamal remains still, a great grin on his face. He nods
and laughs. She is gone.

"What was that?" Ib asks. "A hallucination you've somehow induced in me? Or one of your drama students,

93

acting on your orders. Nothing would surprise me at this point."

Gamal tips back in his chair and a peaceful smile smooths what has until now been a rather maniacal mouth. "I understand your skepticism," he says. "I am the boy who cried Gulf War once too often. But believe me, this is no hallucination. She does not work for the government. She's a member of the Muslim Brotherhood. She dresses this way to avoid harassment. Ironic. European women—and Egyptian women for that matter—dress in Egypt as conservatively as possible to prevent sexual harassment. This good Muslim woman shows her hair, wears jeans, paints her fingernails—but you noticed, no makeup—to avoid political harassment, just as the Muslim Brothers shave their beards in the villages to keep from being beaten by the police all the time."

"What are you talking about?"

Gamal says. "Come along with me at midnight and see for yourself. You'll have the time of your life. You see, I *do* write, for *Al Ahram,* mostly the English edition. Theater reviews. A monthly column. God knows why they asked me to do this. Ruqayyah is just as baffled, despite what she says. I knew the prisoner before his radical fundy days. We used to act together. My wife thinks I'm crazy. If we run into her again tonight, mum's the word. Even George counsels . . ." He waves his hand in front of his face. "But I don't want to talk about that. There's plenty of time. I am interested in this story. When did you do it?" Ib does not understand the question. "How long after I told it did you write it down?"

Ib thinks it was ten minutes. After Gamal ran by the steps of the mosque in that cape. Ib didn't know it was Gamal, consciously. But part of Ib's mind must have recognized him. The moment Gamal ran off the story arrived whole.

"Excellent, very interesting. Are you a writer? I know nothing about you," Gamal says. Ib points out that he hasn't asked. "Forgive me," says Gamal. Ib says he's a historian, and he does some translating.

"Yes, yes, Safeyya said. Do you want to do it again?"

"Do what? No, no I don't." Ib feels awkward once more, like a student in an acting class. "Let's just sit here and not tell any lies. I was beginning to think we were having a real conversation."

"What's a real conversation?" Gamal says dramatically. "You Americans and your fetish of communication. Okay. I see how it works. I'll tell the story, then I'll leave. And someone you think you know will pass by, but not me, and it will turn out to be me. Yes, yes, and you'll need some time—those crucial ten or fifteen minutes. I like how that works."

"No, Gamal. Or is that your real name? Has this entire evening been a practical joke?"

"My full name—and you see, I'm leveling with you here—is Hagop Gamal-Leon Arabian. But I never use the Hagop, just as Charles Robert Redford has dropped his Charles. My parents are both dead. My brothers have all emigrated. I am no longer Armenian." Ib stands up, but he thinks better of this and sits down again. He says he's tired of Gamal's silly stories. Gamal says, "Please bear with me. I'll show you my identification. Listen, here's the bargain. I'll tell you a story, you write it down. Then you tell me one and I'll write it down. All stories will be true. No more joking. We *both* agree to tell no more lies. I mean, come on, who's told more tall tales tonight, you or me?"

Ib does not agree to this scheme. "Okay, how about this," Gamal says. "I tell you a story and you only have to write it down if you feel like it."

Ib shrugs.

Gamal is silent, with a puzzled look on his face, then a faraway look. He says, "I know many songs, but I cannot sing." He pauses. "No, that's not right. Give me a moment."

Ib sits back in his chair, the wicker creaking. He wants a cigarette, but Gamal has his cigarettes.

▲ ▼ ▲ ▼ ▲ ▼ ▲ ▼ ▲ ▼ ▲

After he's finished the story, Gamal stands up. Again the story is a manageable length, but Ib is afraid to say he was not listening to the whole thing. Gamal walks off abruptly and does not look back. Ib watches him as far as the double doors of the old palace. Only a few tables still have people at them. The waiters no longer come out to ask for orders. Ib pays the bill and slips it and the cash into its wooden sleeve on the table. "I could just go home," he says quietly to himself. Home is two blocks away. He yawns. He stretches and when he's done stretching, one hand lands on his notebook. He fingers the well-worn cover. He opens the book. He looks around. No one is watching. He begins to write.

▲ ▼ ▲ ▼ ▲ ▼ ▲ ▼ ▲ ▼ ▲

Gamal returns just as Ib is finishing the story. The reappearance of this man upsets Ib, even though he was expecting him. His heartbeat begins to race. He slumps in his chair and massages his chest. Gamal sits down and waits. Ib's heart rate returns to normal, somewhat normal at least.

He picks up the notebook and reads Gamal's story back to him. Neither of them says a word when he is done. The story appeals to Ib a great deal, but he is afraid to say so, because he thinks it would be vanity. He is not sure how much of it is the story Gamal told him, and how much he made up.

Gamal says simply, "Another?" Ib waits and reminds himself not to listen. Several stories come out this way, each following the rules Gamal set up for the first one.

I Know Many Songs, but I Cannot Sing

The rare daylong rain fell on the Nile valley north of my wife's parents' country home. During the drive south from Cairo, my daughter, Annahíd, asked me to explain the unusual phenomenon several times. It has rained hard twice in her lifetime. I told her that Europe got all this rain every winter, and because the Europeans were rich and thought they still owned the world, they tried to palm their excess precipitation off on us each year, declaring it part of the IMF package Egypt must accept if we expect to receive more loans. My daughter looked as if she were trying to squeeze this information into her brain. The rain ended in the peasant village a few dozen meters from my in-laws' gate. Their man Ramzi waited for us there, pointing to the clean line of clouds that stopped directly over our heads. Then Ramzi indicated the field of alfalfa to the north, where we could see hard wet rain still falling. "You see," I told my daughter, "the Europeans respect your grandfather. They leave his house dry." The sun was shining on the pool and on the grass in the back yard, slanting from the Libyan Desert like the hand of God. Rain had also fallen on the desert, leaving a great swath of pearl-shaped holes. Two officials from the IMF were listening to my father-in-law describe his plans for new middle-class housing in the desert. My daughter and I sat in deck chairs by the pool, patiently awaiting Grandpa's full attention. The four-year-old girl, always busy at something useful, picked pebbles out of a bowl of dried chickpeas. The IMF officials stood on the grass. My father-in-law watered both sand and lawn from a long twitching hose. We knew, even though we could not hear him, that George was insisting Egyptians could learn to love the desert if only their government built living, breathing communities there instead of sterile apartment blocks. The IMF stood with their arms crossed and their chins thrust out at the awful emptiness of the Sahara.

A few days after my wife threw me out the fourth or fifth time, her father began to talk nonstop, mostly in a gentle whisper to himself, sometimes without pausing for breath. I had moved in with my in-laws as I always did. I came in very late one night from play rehearsal to find my mother-in-law at the base of the curving staircase in her nightgown, a candle in her hand, staring up at her husband's study. She described George's mania. I tried to laugh it off, saying we would have more cause to worry if he'd gone silent or if a normally silent man had become suddenly garrulous. She said, "You are absurdly optimistic, Gamal-Leon," sounding for that instant exactly like her daughter. She gave me a parting glance full of some emotional turmoil my shallow mind mistook for sexual longing. When I entered his study, George was talking quietly but dramatically to himself about some Nubian villages whose ingeniously energy-efficient architecture might have been a model for all of Egypt had George only stumbled on them earlier. Just a few days later Lake Nasser swallowed them forever when the High Dam flooded the valley south of Aswan—I'd heard the story many times. George appeared to conclude, saying, "Maupassant used to eat at the restaurant in the Eiffel Tower because it was the only place in Paris where he did not risk seeing the Eiffel Tower. You see?" Then, as if to illustrate this point, he added, "In the desert, the temperature of course is much lower at night, and the cold air remains near the ground during the day if you can keep it in shade. The old Arab towns were built for this, with their narrow streets and alleys hoarding the coolness. But carve rule-straight European boulevards through these old cities, and the wind sucks out the chill. You are left at the mercy of the blazing sun. I have done the same thing to my mind, despite my life's goal of preserving the old Arab ways. I built broad straight boulevards, when I should have followed the winding path of my thoughts. I have failed, Gamal-Leon." George and I were sitting quietly, his head on my shoulder, when the doctor arrived with my wife.

Sleep was always the enemy when I was growing up. We lived in a noisy, crowded district of Cairo, where the neighbors' arguments were easier to solve than our own. The cafés my brothers and I frequented were open all night. When I was very young, I put my bedding on the wide windowsill to eavesdrop on the Blue Nile coffeehouse. My eldest brother favored this haunt, where joy for life and love of coffee seemed one and the same thing. The nightly celebrations turned to mumbles and yawns only when the sun brushed the sky and the men in the café glared at the streaks of gray in their narrow strip of heaven. Ramadan was the happiest time of my year, even though we were Christian and fatherless. Everyone in the city joined me in my war against sleep, at least while it was dark. Women and children also stayed up late then, parading through the streets in search of sweets and pancakes and ribbons of delicate dough spun off domes of red-hot metal. My wife, years later, stubbornly slept through the night for the month after our baby was born. That first month coincided with Ramadan, and I would sit on the balcony with a small lantern, reading, writing, or taking notes on the neighbors' conversations at parties I could practically touch. The baby would make her tentative gurgles and talk to her thumb, and I would go inside to roll my still-sleeping wife onto her side. I would free her beautiful breasts and bring the baby to its target, both heartwarming parenting and erotic torture. But my wife usually surfaced, irritated that her sleep was being sucked from her, angry with the neighbors for their pagan revelry until all hours, and annoyed with me for enjoying my insomnia. The introduction of American baby formula to our markets allowed my wife to sleep till morning. My father died one night when I was too young to remember. Except I do remember staying up very late with my brothers, enjoying what my young mind mistook for a happy party, finally falling asleep at dawn with the rosy sense that love was something you found only at the end of a long night of wakefulness.

One night before bed I was telling my daughter an old Armenian fairy tale, acting out several parts and speaking in Armenian. I used props to turn myself into different characters: her security blanket for a mountain lion; the wire mesh wastebasket for the king. With my own Basque beret I became the court jester whose jokes and playlets no one wanted to hear anymore. Annahíd, a sigh away from sleep, sat upright at this character. She stretched and, as she yawned, brought three fingers daintily down over her mouth, just as her mother did. "Daddy. You aren't supposed to be in this story. It happened a long time ago. How did you get into the story?" Then she curled up and drifted off to sleep. I continued to whisper the tale, entranced as it seemed to unravel on its own. She began to snore, a signal she was feigning sleep and wanted me to leave. But I was debating whether to write this story down, sell it in America, get film rights. The problem was my Armenian tales did not translate well into English or Arabic. They lost their alpine grace and playfulness. I told them in Armenian because my Coptic Egyptian wife refused to learn the language. My daughter understood but did not speak it. I also used Armenian to turn the terrible arguments my wife and I had into funny stories. I whispered goodnight in French and left the room. A few steps out the door, I heard my daughter's reply, in the Armenian phrase that began all my bedtime stories to her: "I know many songs, but I cannot sing." I dashed back to the doorway, but she was asleep. I could tell by her breathing, a delicate whistle, not the pretend snoring she had made earlier.

"*Ayza* some *badi*," she had a habit of saying around the age of two. *Ayza* means "I want." *Badi*, pronounced "body," is short for *zabadi*, "yogurt." We thought this was adorable. She was mixing Arabic and English, but also making a play on words. She meant, early in the morning, that she wanted some yogurt for breakfast. But she also meant that she wanted *somebody* to play with, or perhaps some *body* to keep her warm, just a body. She repeated this performance dozens of mornings in a row until it was no longer funny, but it was always funny on its own terms. We made the mistake of mentioning it to Wael Barakat, our good friend, Annahíd's godfather, and head of the Euro-American Advertising Agency in Cairo. Wael decided to use the three words for a television ad campaign, which he was preparing for Nestlé, makers of the yogurt rich Egyptians and expatriates were eating. Euro-American Advertising always used blond Euro-American models to

105

sing—dubbed in—catchy tunes that mixed Arabic and English, sometimes in the same word. My wife fought Wael like a Hollywood agent for the rights to this phrase, which she copyrighted under his nose the day we had the argument with him over it, by mailing off a postcard to ourselves with the sentence written on it, followed by the copyright symbol. There is no such fastidiousness about patented ideas in Egypt, but Wael loved to mimic all sorts of American behavior. We made ten thousand Egyptian pounds. By the time the commercial arrived on television, over a year later, Annahíd was speaking in long complex sentences. When she saw the ad, she burst into tears. She said, "I was never that young, Baba. I feel very used." We were alarmed by the last word. We asked if she felt we had exploited her. She knew what "exploited" meant. "No, no, no," she said. "I am not that little girl anymore. She's been used up. She's all gone now. A long time ago, she was used up. I am very old now, you have no idea how old I am."

In a dream my daughter Annahíd felt her mother pull one arm and say, "This child is as Egyptian as the sand under the Step Pyramid." Her daddy took the other arm, with a tug, and said, "But this limb feels as Armenian as Aslan, the mountain lion who ate only unbelievers."

They held each arm firmly. They pulled. The noise of
Annahíd coming apart was surprisingly soft, a gentle
pop. Now there were two Annahíds. But one Annahíd
awoke hugging herself, very sad she was not twins. She
got up and dressed all by herself. It was dark. As she
walked down the hall to the dining room she realized
her tee shirt was on backwards. Tears welled up in her
eyes. She was a girl who liked things in their proper
place and threw a fit at the merest hint of chaos. But the
feeling of the shirt on backwards was so like being
pulled apart that the tears soon dried. The sun was beginning to wake, but like Annahíd it had sleep in its
eyes, a fog that obscured even the balcony of the building next door, where the big American men laughed too
loud and did not sweep the dust. Annahíd found her
parents in the kitchen at the corner of the big metal
table Cook chopped chickens on. My wife and I sat on
tall stools. We looked funny there, shoulders scrunched
up, eyes practically droozed asleep, holding hands! An
unschooled observer might assume we were happy ever
after. But Annahíd knew we were simply too tired to argue anymore about which school to send her to: the
German language school (my choice) or the Arabic (my
wife's). Annahíd left the doorway. It is hard to say
whether my wife or I actually saw her. My balcony gar-

den beckoned, my exotic African plants. Annahíd stood in the swirl of smells. Deh-deh, our maid, would not arrive for another hour, too long. A plant spoke to her: "Eat me."

"But what if you are poison?" she said.

"You read *Alice in Wonderland* all by yourself and you're only four years old," said the plant. "You know how the story turns out."

We live next door to an American oil exploration company. I sit out on my balcony overlooking the Nile in the morning before the sun rises too high and sip my wife's exquisite Turkish coffee and listen to the general manager of the oil company argue with his partner. I watch them arrive every morning in sparkling clean identical red Jeep Cherokees. They live a few blocks from each other in the same suburb, but it never occurs to them to ride together in one vehicle. Both are huge men in the shoulders and chest with skinny legs. One is from Denver, the other from Fort Worth. Denver and Fort Worth disagree over just about everything, but most often about how to treat Egyptians, both at the office and in the field. Denver is no Lawrence of Arabia, but he does speak kindly to his staff and has even made a friend of his chief surveyor, Gaber, a master at computers and a genius at keeping the machines alive despite the fickle currents of Egyptian electricity. Fort Worth calls Egyptians "wogs" behind their backs. He rails against their circular thinking and their endless coffee breaks. But he is afraid to be in the building alone with them. One morning Fort Worth was on the phone to Denver, who was home with food poisoning. I was less than five feet from Denver's desk, which Fort Worth appropriates whenever his partner is absent, feeling maybe he is safer in the kinder man's office. Denver also has a balcony, dusty from disuse. Our buildings are side by side facing the Nile, and it is an easy crawl from my balcony. Fort Worth had been alone in the office two hours that day, calling Denver often and with increasingly pathetic and inconsequential questions. Denver hung up on him the last time, but I could tell—don't ask how—that Fort Worth kept talking to a dead line. He was confiding to the dial tone that the key to preventive medicine in Egypt was to drink an American beer with the juice of one lemon before every meal, even breakfast. I slipped onto his balcony and studied him through the blinds. He had painted half of the black telephone with Wite-Out, the now obsolete correcting fluid.

H. Kimball Johnson of Fort Worth, Texas, was at his office next door to our apartment very early that morning because of an overnight flight from Kuwait. I reconstruct all this from a few laconic sentences he told me. Instead of going home to Ma'adi—Johnson was too keyed up to sleep—he went directly to Zamalek. Then, as he was spreading out a map of a south Sinai oilfield, the odor of ambergris wafted in through the window. Johnson does not have an acute sense of smell. Apparently that's his wife Leslee's department. Inside her airtight BMW she can detect a cigarette being smoked in the car ahead of them at sixty miles an hour. This is why the scent so upset Kimball Johnson: the woman next to him on the plane from Kuwait had shown him a nugget of ambergris during a forgettable conversation. This lump of whale intestinal matter set something off deep in Johnson. Before smelling it, he had been only partly involved in the conversation with the bookseller from London (his mind was also comparing equipment replacement costs using Bombay versus Piraeus suppliers). The instant after a whiff of this powerful, sweet, sexy, rancid odor—like roses and Play-doh—his attention focused completely on his neighbor. She was not all that pretty. She had a large horsey face, her skin wasn't good, hair thin and wispy, hips too wide for Johnson's taste, which ran, in his private and pathetic fantasies, to very young teenage girls. But with an intensity he'd never before experienced—he had not once in his marriage even considered cheating on Leslee—he found himself wounded to the quick by this British woman's beauty and charm and indirectness. Nothing happened. They parted with a tepid handshake, without exchanging names. Then, from his partner's office, he smelled the musky ambergris again. Something told him to act. He had never been out on the balcony before. For a moment a dust storm on the horizon distracted him. Somewhere nearby was what sounded like a creaking shutter, but there was no wind. Finally he spied on the floor of the balcony next door the twisted, convulsing body of my daughter, vomiting but otherwise strangely quiet. Johnson bounded across the terrifying abyss of five floors and scooped up the little girl, grabbed the half-eaten leaf beside her, and thundered into the many-roomed apartment looking for us. His big Jeep took the three of us to the American hospital. His connections and intimidating American presence sped us past the bureaucracy of the front desk into the emergency room. Then it was as if it had never happened. My wife and Annahíd were asleep in the hospital room, and Kimball Johnson was asking me why he might have smelled ambergris on my daughter. Her clothes were draped over my arm. I lifted her tee shirt, and my little blue plastic vial of ambergris fell to the floor. "She must have nicked it from my bathroom this morning," I said. "I used some after shaving last night before we went to a party." Her little body had crushed the container when she fell. Opened even a crack, the scent fills the air. Humans can smell one millionth of a part a dozen feet away because it so closely resembles human pheromones. Kimball Johnson was crying. In a hoarse whisper, he said, "You will surely despise me, but I might have left her laying there, had her skirt not shimmied up her bottom when she fell. She didn't have any panties on. I would be lying, sir, if I said I jumped onto your balcony only to save her life."

Charles Mattimore is on his hands and knees scrubbing the balcony floor where my daughter vomited, even though our maid had cleaned it up immediately. We are returning from the hospital dazed. As it happens, we arrive at cocktail hour. Charles has opened a bottle of Bordeaux. Three of our best crystal wineglasses sit beside the bottle of wine. We lock the cabinet these wineglasses are in so that not even our most trusted servant can get at them. I pick up one glass and exchange glances with

Safeyya, whose eyes tell me she did not give him the key
either. Charles stands up, straightening his pants, and
says, "Go ahead. The wine has been breathing for half
an hour. It's not absurdly expensive, but I think you'll
find it quite passable." I pour two glasses, one for
Safeyya, one for myself. Charles says mildly, "Aren't you
having some, Gamal-Leon? This isn't out of dubious sympathy for your Mohammedan brothers?" He takes both
glasses and hands one to Safeyya, who sits down too
suddenly with hers. But Charles has stopped time,
reached out, and snatched her falling wineglass from the
air. All three of us watch the rough seas within the crystal gradually subside. Not a drop has been spilled.
Charles returns the wine to Safeyya. I have not, before
this moment, realized what an astonishing beauty my
wife is. Safeyya thanks Charles but raises a hand to her
mouth as if she's burped. I pour another glass for myself.
Charles Mattimore and I sit simultaneously. I suppose we
are waiting for him to mention some trivial aspect of my
daughter's brush with death. He raises his glass. "A
toast," he says. "Have you heard the news? Paraguay's
Stroessner was deposed today. The last of the true fascists. To a great general!" My eyes must be as wide as
Safeyya's are. I feel a sob trapped deep inside my chest.
We ignore his toast. We drink the wine. He is hurt by this

snub. But the wine's taste dazzles me. Safeyya holds her glass with both hands, as if praying to the wine. We drink very slowly, not speaking. Charles drinks deliberately too, but distractedly, as if he were not drinking the finest wine he's ever tasted. He says something finally, and I am not listening. I don't know why, but I ask him to repeat himself. He says, "I visited Paraguay once. What wonderful highways and railroads. It is true what they say of the fascists. Hitler gave fascism a bad name. I stopped one night at a little pension in the mountains. Charming efficient German service in the middle of all that Latin American chaos and incivility. The proprietor was German but he spoke Spanish with me, and when I told him my surname, he said, 'Matamoras. It means "kill the Moors."' I lied to him that my father's ancestors were indeed Spanish. We became fast friends." Charles Mattimore pours more wine for Safeyya, for me. He has tears in his eyes. I put my glass down and rise and place both hands gently around his neck. He stares up with the same terrible wounded look Annahíd sometimes has. He has been watching her closely. He is too interested in Annahíd. "Pack your bags," I say. "And be gone by ten-thirty tomorrow morning." Then I weaken: "We'll call a few friends. See if they can put you up."

I KNOW MANY SONGS, BUT I CANNOT SING

▲ ▼ ▲ ▼ ▲ ▼ ▲ ▼ ▲ ▼ ▲

Ib and Gamal are at the Atlas Zamalek Hotel in Mohandiseen. The theme music from the old television show "Dallas" plays over the intercom. They are pausing on the way to visit Lena's flat in nearby Agouza, which she still keeps now three years after having married Yehya and moved into his Giza high-rise. She uses the Agouza apartment to write her doctoral thesis, a project she has been working on for seven years. When she finishes it, she'll be done with her career. There are no jobs in her field in Egypt. Yehya will not move to the U.S. or Europe because he works exclusively in Arabic. So she keeps writing and unwriting her thesis. Gamal and Ib saw an Argentine friend of Lena's at the Marriott, who told them about the improvised evening. A small event, without Yehya, who is going to a theater party in Heliopolis, the reason Lena decided to throw a competing party of her own. Ib and Gamal stopped at the Atlas Zamalek and called her, to make sure it was okay to visit now. They are sitting in the lobby, because she asked them to give her fifteen minutes.

A pair of Egyptian men and a European woman wait for the elevator to take them to the discotheque on the top floor. The men are holding each other's pinky fingers.

The woman is talking to them but looking at Ib. The irritating way she lets her hair fall across her face reminds Ib of Lena. "What," he says to Gamal, "would you think of setting me up with Lena?"

Gamal makes a noise like a camel being shoved into a butcher's truck. He jumps to his feet. "Don't joke about that. I forbid you even to entertain the fantasy." He starts off, toward the side exit.

"Why?" Ib hurries to keep up. "Because she's married? I know, I know. It's not right. I don't like the idea either. But something tells me their marriage is on the rocks." He has not told Gamal of his encounter with Lena earlier in the evening. Recalling their kiss causes a brief blinding flash of something in his brain, like the memory of magnesium exploding into flame.

They are on the street. They cross a wide boulevard and turn into a slender alley. They do not speak for a few blocks. They come to the old neighborhood of Agouza. They pass down an even narrower and suddenly very dark street. Exposed brick. Buildings lean over the street. The sickly sweet smell of urine hangs in the air, but Ib is elated. Ten years ago this was the village of Agouza, surrounded by fields, a rural suburb of Cairo. The city swallowed the small town whole but left it strangely untouched. Perhaps Cairo did not like the taste of Agouza. Broad confident avenues go lanky and crooked here. Lena avoids the neighborhood, especially at night. She used to walk here, thinking it was quaint and archaeologically interesting, but men would speak words at her that made her say, "What would your mother think?"

"I am sorry I played that joke about Nur on you," Gamal says. "I see it has only made you long for Lena. She is a very beautiful woman. But she is also a good woman, and they have a happy marriage, unlike for instance my own marriage. I would be very happy—well, not happy, but perhaps pleased somewhere in my soul to relinquish Safeyya to . . . well, not to you, of course. You are not her type. But I very much object to the idea of interfering with a happy marriage, even if it is only an idle fantasy on your part. You can be forgiven for this, however. You do not know them well."

Ib is challenged by this, fascinated by a streak of morality he did not expect to find in the maze of Gamal's personality. "What if I told you Lena and I kissed this evening," Ib says, "right in front of Yehya? And he ap-

117

plauded. You saw us sitting in the theater. You must have noticed how it was between us. The kiss came out of nowhere, neither of us initiated it. I think she's as surprised as I was by our attraction. Maybe it's because you and I have become friends. She kept saying how much she admires you."

"Oh, bullshit. I scare her because I act as if there were no social rules. I wish I knew the rules, but I am an alien and no one will teach me, not my wife, not my daughter." They round a corner onto another narrow dirt street, and the darkness is blasted away by bright blue light—a rectangular stall where two men with lace caps iron shirts on high boards. A television with a gaping hole in one side nevertheless shows the fuzzy image of a local soccer match. The *makhwagi* watch the game intently and iron without looking down, the various elements of their work spread out around them— piles of shirts, cups of water to spit-spray the shirts, the two types of irons. "What's the score?" Gamal asks in Arabic. He stops to catch the game, makes himself at home on the lone customer chair. Ib has to stand.

The older man says with disgust, "Ahli is victorious for the moment, but Zamalek will overcome the deficit and triumph by two goals." Ib is touched by the fellow's fussy classical Arabic and by the interest in a game that was played several weeks ago. During Ramadan there are no matches.

Gamal jumps to his feet. He says, "These men have no idea what I am, foreigner or *baladi,* rich or poor." He's speaking English, a language they do not understand, but Ib nevertheless feels dismayed it's being done in front of them. Gamal continues, "They are always impressed by my courtesy. The upper class looks right past men like these two, as if they were furniture. Don't get me wrong, I don't mind it, but sometimes I think both classes see right through me. Look at how *you* saw me at first this evening. We work in the same small university. We've probably crossed paths there dozens of times, and yet you could not imagine me as anything but a bumpkin. You thought I was playing a practical joke on you, but in fact *you* created the character. I just stayed in character. Actually, being invisible is an aid to my art. Most people think I don't understand Arabic unless I speak it first." They leave the shop.

"Gamal, you talk as if you're an outsider in this city, but you're not."

Gamal laughs and says, "You hardly understand the language, let alone the customs, the hidden signals, the texture of conversation. I can tell you guess what people are saying in Arabic most of the time, and you're right much more often than not, but in the end you can't even read a half-Egyptian like Lena." Yet he claps Ib on the shoulder and a moment later says, "You are pulling my leg about Lena. I deserve it, no question."

"Believe what you wish. Just watch how she greets me."

Gamal takes a shortcut through a tire repair shop which has a huge tree growing in the middle of it. The building must have been constructed around the tree. Tires hang on rods screwed into the trunk. Gamal nods to a boy sitting on a pair of tires, and he exits by a small green door, onto another street, the outer edge of the old village of Agouza. This feels to Ib like a gate through time, moving from the thousand-year-old village to the ten-year-old apartment buildings and Bauhaus villas.

Gamal says, "There are certain marriages I want to believe in. Lena and Yehya's marriage is one of those. I depend on their stability." Ib says he was only joking.

He is tired of the subject but can't help wondering aloud that if a wife can be seduced, isn't it a sign that the marriage was already in bad shape? "I don't want to argue about this," Gamal says. "But I must insist. You are our guest in this country. I order you not to—"

"Why? Am I so offensive?"

"No, ho no." The emotion in Gamal-Leon's voice surprises Ib. Gamal says, "I like you very much. Safeyya adores you. She is plotting and scheming as we speak to marry you off to some friend so we can keep you here, trap you in Egypt. Don't be flattered. It is a grim life we have planned for you."

They pass a leather-faced man in a galabiya and turban, who is selling olives and pens on the street. A static-filled squawking issues from him, and the man reaches into the folds of his galabiya and pulls out a walky-talky. Gamal says, "The police are everywhere. It's called the City Eye system. People aren't as frightened as they were under Sadat or Nasser, but in fact they're dangerously lulled into a feeling that this regime is incompetent, basically good-hearted. Personally I am glad so many of my conversations are being recorded.

121

When I'm an old man, I'll use the records like ancient journals, perhaps write my autobiography. It's reassuring to know that someday I'll understand what was going on in my life."

Ib decides to attack illogic with more nonsense. "I stopped by the girls' dorm at the American University last spring and left a note," he says. "I wrote it there in the lobby—for a woman I was infatuated with—"

Gamal says, "We aren't finished with Lena."

Ib says, "Let me tell you something for once. I wrote the note with my red paper-grading pen as the woman at the desk watched. An irrelevant detail, you might think. But the next day I ran into another student of mine, an Egyptian woman who grew up in Buffalo, New York, who thinks we are much better pals than we are, and she said there was a rumor going around campus that I'd left a message for a student at the girls' hostel which I wrote with red lipstick."

"Red lipstick," Gamal repeats, laughing. "I think I heard that story."

"And shortly afterwards, I ran into a colleague who teaches philosophy—your friend Charles Mattimore, actually. He said he'd been standing in a crowd on a busy street corner when paramilitary police jumped out of a van and gunned down a fundamentalist. Charles was standing as close to the guy as you are to me. He noticed two things about him. The dead man was making unmistakable come-hither eye contact with him, the instant before the shooting, and the blood smeared on his face after the shooting looked like lipstick badly applied."

"Charles witnessed that assassination? He never told us," Gamal says. "I'm amazed Charles could keep such a lurid tale to himself. He must not have told anyone but you, because a good story spreads like gonorrhea in this town."

They arrive at Lena's building. She answers the door in a bathrobe, her hair wild, her body visible under the silk. "I said give me a half hour. No one is *arrivé* yet. Wait, wait." She runs down the hallway into the flat. They wait. Pots clatter, cabinet doors slam. Ib says, "Well, I'm going in. We can help set up." Gamal-Leon takes Ib by the wrist and yanks him backwards. "No," he says. "This is not done. We'll walk around the block and come back in fifteen minutes." Ib agrees, but the instant Gamal lets go of his arm, he bolts down the hall into the apartment.

Lena is in her study, humming to herself, the door ajar an inch. Eventually, Gamal tiptoes into the flat.

They find Lena's servant Ahmad talking angrily with himself in the kitchen. Ib knows Ahmad hates working here, considers it a demotion from their more opulent Nile-side Giza apartment. But that is not why he's muttering to himself. "He's bonkers," Lena confessed once. She thinks Yehya is too lenient with their servants. Ahmad grabs Gamal's elbow and points to a corner of the kitchen wall, saying, *"Bursa, bursa."* Ib whispers, "What's that?" Gamal says, "A rare poisonous lizard that spits venom at its victims."

Following a short conference, Gamal and Ahmad chase around the flat after imaginary *bursa,* squealing and laughing, wildly swinging a tool designed for this purpose (a two-meter-long pole with a brush at one end). What they find are harmless geckos.

▲ ▼ ▲ ▼ ▲ ▼ ▲ ▼ ▲ ▼ ▲

Lena sits sideways in the sling-back chair, her hair wet. Her loose blouse flaps in the breeze, revealing from time to time a lacy black bra strap. This is unusual behavior. Lena seems at ease, a little sleepy. Ib has never seen her so calm before a party. He has never known her to sit sideways in a chair. Her damp skin has left a design on her blouse: a *V* shape between her breasts. Ib watches the pulse in her neck. "My doctor took me off my prescription for artificial thyroid for the time being," she says in a low sexy voice. "Did you guys know I have a defective thyroid gland? So I'm kinda loopy." She is arranging a bowl of crackers and cheese and olives with one hand. The crackers form a *Y*. Ib interprets this *Y* as an unconscious *You*. She speaks again: "Yehya went to dinner in Heliopolis." Ib blushes at the thought: *Yehya*. *Y* is for *Yehya*. Lena continues, "He didn't want me to go so for a while I wanted nothing more in the world than to go to this stupid director's house. But tonight I recognized I would not have a terrific time there. It would be full of actors posturing, people like Gamal-Leon, only worse. So I decided, on the spur of the moment—is that the phrase? What does 'spur' mean, like a Western? I decided to make a terrific

125

party myself without telling Yehya." She laughs, not her usual high-speed warble, but a hoarse, deep-throated rumble. "I called a woman whose husband is also going to this party in Heliopolis, and she loved the idea. She called more friends. So that's how this happened. I can see you're very interested. I am sorry to bore you. Have I been talking too much?"

"Which director?" Gamal asks. He stands up and walks to the kitchen. "Yusef Shahine," she says. Gamal barks. He says, "You're turning down an opportunity to spend an evening with Shahine? Why didn't Yehya tell me about this party?" Lena laughs luxuriously again.

"What have you two been doing since I saw you?" she asks. This too is against type: Lena never changes the subject. Ib is not sure he likes this Lena as much, although he finds her intensely sexy tonight, her tangled jungle of unbrushed hair, the soft dark down on her arms.

Gamal is chipping ice with a hammer and Ahmad is chattering at him. Gamal answers, "We've been writing a novel. Show her, Ib."

"Be serious," Lena says, but she taps Ib on the knee. She says to Gamal, "Have you been to the hospital today?"

"We just came from the hospital," Gamal shouts. The lie sounds so sincere Ib wonders for a moment if Gamal means that earlier in the evening he went to the hospital. Gamal says, "She's fine, right as rain. She asked Uncle Ib to tell her a story but then she kept correcting him, changing the story, demanding a better plot."

Gamal has come into the room and he's waving the hammer about as he talks. Ib grabs the hammer. Ib says, "We have not just come from the hospital. We're going to go later. But should we go now—for visiting hours?"

"You're not my conscience," Gamal says. "You're my scribe."

Lena says, "I talked with Safeyya an hour ago. Annahíd is asleep. She said there is no point going until morning. But she was speaking of *my* going. Gamal-Leon, I don't mean to lecture, but you ought to visit your daughter."

127

Gamal giggles, as if Lena has just told the punch line of a joke. He is so good at mimicking other people's laughs it is impossible to tell if this is his own or an imitation. "Show her the novel, Ib. Did I tell you we were writing a novel, Lena?"

"Shut up, Gamal," Lena says. Ib stands and wanders over to a bookshelf and fingers a copy of Washington Irving's biography of Mohammad. Lena follows Ib and nudges him toward her study. "There's a chapter of my doctoral thesis on the desk," she says. "Would you mind reading it?"

Ib closes the door and sits on the bed. From time to time, he can hear Lena whisper to arriving guests, "Leave Ib alone. He's reading my thesis." He does not even try to read her thesis, which is about the Egyptian intellectuals Mohammad Ali sent to study Europe in the early nineteenth century. Ib browses through his journal and Gamal's stories. The fascinating thing about writing down these stories was how Ib assumed Gamal's voice and personality. This has never happened to Ib before. He has always considered himself a poor mimic and a bad listener.

Lena enters the room after only ten minutes. "Have you read it? What do you think?"

Ib says, "I couldn't concentrate. Let me read you one of the stories Gamal told me." Lena sighs but agrees to listen. She settles onto the bed and Ib is electrified by her closeness. He reads her the story of how Annahíd ate the poison plant.

She is silent for a moment afterwards, pulling her left ring finger with her right hand. "She did it on purpose?" Lena says slowly. "That can't be true. Safeyya would have told me. No, Gamal is blowing this thing out of proportion. Or he's lying to you. But that is not how Gamal-Leon usually dramatizes things. He does not exaggerate. He takes on a wholly new character. No, I don't believe a four-year-old would try to kill herself."

▲ ▼ ▲ ▼ ▲ ▼ ▲ ▼ ▲ ▼ ▲

A pizza arrives in the middle of the party. "Who ordered it?" Ib asks the man who delivers it. The pizza man grins and says, "Nobody." Then he says, "I am Gaber." Ib pictures Gaber, an enterprising young man, sitting in his

129

narrow empty restaurant, watching a steady stream of well-dressed *khawagas* go to Lena's building. Gaber has an idea: he'll make a pizza and take it over, and no one will be the wiser. "Business is slow tonight, *mish kidda?*" Ib says, fishing out the pound notes. Gaber smiles brightly, showing off healthy teeth. Unembarrassed, he takes Ib's money. Perfume precedes a woman coming up the stairs, and she slips chastely past Gaber, saying softly, *"Shokran, ya Gaber."* She has money ready for him and Gaber is about to take her payment, too, with an innocent glance directly at Ib meant to confuse him momentarily. But Ib reaches over and pats Gaber's hand. "I paid him," Ib says. She looks up at him—this is Ruqayyah wearing a head scarf, the Muslim *hegab.* "Why did you pay him?" she asks. "*I* ordered the pizza." Ib does not know what to say. Between the time Ib and Ruqayyah met earlier in the evening and now, Ib overheard a stray remark at the party, from two strangers, which supplied Gamal-Leon's sister-in-law with a name, also Ruqayyah. But it never occurred to him to connect the two Ruqayyahs, this one from the Marriott and the faceless entity, Safeyya's sister Ruqayyah. It is impossible that Coptic Christian Safeyya would have a Muslim sister. Gaber grabs Ruqayyah's money and darts down the stairs. "I'll get him," Ib says. But Ruqayyah takes Ib's hand, pulling him into the party. They leave the pizza in the kitchen. Ruqayyah leads Ib, still by the hand, to Lena's study. She tugs at her scarf and, looking directly into Ib's eyes, slips it off her head as if in prelude to a striptease. They sit on the bed. Ib is entranced. "Are you Safeyya's sister?" he asks. Ruqayyah nods, eyes still locked on Ib's. "Were you pulling my leg at the Marriott?" She shakes her head. She has a beautiful, sympathetic smile. Ib can see the resemblance to Safeyya and Hanaa, the slender face, the gray expressive eyes.

"I was married to the prisoner you'll be interviewing," she says. "He was the reason I converted, although I did not believe in Islam when he and I were married. After we divorced, I was drawn into a Sufi group and my real conversion began." Ib says he won't be going to the interview, because (1) he does not believe this prisoner exists, and (2) if one did, it would be foolish for an American to go . . . Ruqayyah laughs sweetly and leans over and kisses Ib on the cheek. "You have been talking too long with Gamal-Leon. It is a good thing I came to this soirée. You need another perspective, and a much prettier one at that!"

131

Ib asks Ruqayyah which tariqa of Sufis she belongs to. Perhaps he knows them.

"Oh, Ib. I've heard a lot about you. You are known to our sheikh, considered a perfect candidate for conversion because of all this business of exile and alienation. And yet you've never actually been seduced by the light. But then I too was considered an impossible case. A convert to Islam is a dagger through the heart of the Coptic Church. My father does not know where one Coptic church is in Cairo, but he would not speak to me for three years. My sister still won't speak to me, but only because she's jealous. She realizes I've found a home in Egypt, after all these centuries. Every Copt has a bag packed, ready to flee at a moment's notice, although we claim to be the original Egyptians. Safeyya is wrong that I've found home, but I would not dream of telling her." Ruqayyah rifles through her small purse and finds her lipstick. Slowly, carefully, without a mirror, she reapplies the pink lipstick. Her face is so close to Ib's it is as if she were using him instead of a mirror.

▲ ▼ ▲ ▼ ▲ ▼ ▲ ▼ ▲ ▼ ▲

The room vibrates gently. Lena is crouched changing tapes, but the tape she puts into the cassette player sounds exactly the same as the tape that just ended: Moroccan mountain music. "Isn't it great?" she says to no one in particular. Ib spies a soft empty chair on the far side of the large living room. He slips through the crowd, twisting sideways here and there, ducking to avoid a generous arm gesture. When he arrives at his chair, two young Palestinian women have occupied it, whispering like a pair of lovers. How does he know they are Palestinian? It's only a guess, but they have been gossiping with each other all evening, avoiding the other women in the room, isolated by the homelessness their minds lay over all human interaction they have. He steps out onto the balcony. A rubber-leafed flame tree bends several branches over the balcony, and flowers, engorged by their own fertility, fall in a shower of succulent petals on Ib's head. He sits with a thump in the hard wicker chair. "Stephen, isn't it?" says a voice from the darkness to his right. Ib knows the voice, doesn't bother to look at the dim figure. "Charles," Ib says. "It's Ib, it's me." Charles Mattimore laughs tepidly. "Don't confuse me, Stephen. You were telling me the other day about your recent trip to Siwa where the local sheikhs still trade in young teenage boys. You bought one yourself, but the station chief in Alex made you exchange him for a rug." Ib strikes a match to light his cigarette, and he briefly uses the flame to illuminate his face. Charles says, "Ib! How awkward. Why didn't you say so?"

Ib laughs and says, "Gamal-Leon and I have been writing stories about you tonight. I thought it only fair to warn you. They're good, so you'll have to expect to be exposed at last. You will never practice your peculiar brand of gynecology in the Middle East again." Charles Mattimore is uncharacteristically silent. Then he says, as if carefully choosing his words, "You're not truly writing about me?" Ib can hear him swallowing.

▲ ▼ ▲ ▼ ▲ ▼ ▲ ▼ ▲ ▼ ▲

Charles Mattimore blows smoke rings on the cramped balcony of Lena's flat. Behind them, inside, the party is at full speed. Lena is playing Prince now, a bootleg tape that pops and hisses. Ib feels the steady thumping of dancers behind him. On the rooftop of the apartment building across the interior courtyard is another party, an Egyptian gathering. Lena's party has many Egyptians, but most are non-Egyptian: Dutch, English, Belgian, Australian, Jordanian, Palestinian. The Egyptians Lena invites are expatriates within their own country, like Yehya, who grew up in London and Madrid. Charles comments that there are no Americans at Lena's get-together. He pauses after he says this, like a weary comedian, and then says, "Except for you, Ib." Ib does not respond. Charles launches into one of his vaguely comic, mostly irritating attacks on Americans, how they talk in conversation to whole rooms, their annoying shoes and shorts, their politicians, their propensity to remark "Oh my God!," which Charles delivers in a flat nasal American accent. Then another pause and he says, "But you're not *American*, Ib. You don't abuse your children with one hand and run for Congress with the other. You've never been on a chat show to deny that you can hold your breath underwater for five minutes." Noise from the party indoors and the one across the way picks up, mixing interestingly. People chant at the rooftop Egyptian party next door. Everyone smokes cigarettes, at both parties.

Gamal startles both Ib and Charles by speaking quietly from the corner of the balcony, as though he's been standing there listening for some time. "They are celebrating the birth of a boy tonight over there. It is the holiest night of Ramadan, when the archangel Gabriel first whispered the word of God to Mohammad. Women induce labor today if at all possible. They are telling prophetic stories about this child as a grown man, very rare for the middle classes, who fear the evil eye, who never speak of a child's future to avoid scrutiny by djinns. But a child born tonight is supposed to rule the world. He will go on 'Oprah' and make her sob with joy at her religious awakening. He will kill men like Charles with just a thought."

The party is in a lull state. One set of guests has left, so only a dozen people remain, some in the kitchen, a few on the balcony. The tape deck is not playing, and a call to prayer outdoors is audible over women ululating at the *baladi* party across the interior courtyard. Lena walks around the room at one point reminding everyone that more guests are due, any minute, don't leave yet. She has put on a silk bathrobe over her blouse and black pants. Conversations are spasmodic, intermittent. People seem to be forgetting what they are saying in the middle of saying it. Charles Mattimore takes advantage of this indolence to lecture everyone on the balcony and in the living room on life in Cairo. There are a few murmured asides: "But he doesn't live here anymore." "He's been asked by the government to leave again, but the American University is shielding him because he has important documents." Charles ignores these remarks. He says the metaphor for existence here is Oasis and Desert. Indeed all things of value in the twentieth century necessarily have to reside in an oasis, and they are threatened by a desert of ignorance, depravity, ugliness, and barbarism. In all of Egypt, he says, there are only five people who know how to live a civilized life. Someone from the living room shouts, "Here, here!" Charles continues, after clearing his throat: "And none of them is at this party." A Danish painter walks onto the balcony and pauses over a former lover of his, a woman from Canada or New Zealand, and he says of Charles Mattimore, to her but for everyone to hear, "Isn't that the fellow who invented the telegraph?" Everyone laughs. People from the kitchen call, "What was the joke?" and it is repeated for them. Charles wears a very tight starched collar and a bow tie. He lightly fingers the bow tie, as if about to undo it. He reveals no facial response to this devastating comic deflation. He is indeed out of place in the twentieth century.

Ib tells Charles some of the complaints Gamal-Leon has lodged against Ib so far this long evening: He is lazy, too

137

serious, too silly, an unhip dresser; he doesn't sing or use his diaphragm to project his voice; he can't really get his mouth around a foreign language; he is self-involved; he has indulged in a cult of private mythologies, is pampered, self-protected, has never lived a grown-up life and gotten a real job and established a place for himself in the world, is smug with the love of three parents (while Gamal barely had one), is too sure love happens; he inspires others to help him—to offer him hospitality, bed, time, food. It is as if it would be cruel not to. Is Ib aware of this? Is it unconscious or conscious? Charles Mattimore, illuminated from his corner of the balcony only by the red dot of his cigarette, says, "These are all valid critiques of your soapy American personality, Ib. But by the way you spoke them we might presume they are *self*-criticisms, another peculiarly American trait. You so cleverly condemn yourselves and your countrymen, you take the fun out of it for the rest of us." The music has stopped inside, and there is silence, save for the soft crackle of Cleopatra cigarettes. Gamal says, "Your Mario Cuomo says he runs for office in poetry and governs in prose. Those earlier remarks of mine—if I said them— were poetry." Ib remembers his nephew at the funeral in Massachusetts tugging at his sleeve, saying, "If you were really in Egypt why don't you smell like Egypt?"

Ib tells a story to discredit Charles, whom he suspects witnessed crucial moments of Annahíd's crisis.

"I sat a few chairs away from Charles Mattimore the other day in the campus courtyard. He did not see me, or if he had he wasn't speaking to me. I had not responded to his letter suggesting I put him up for a week or two in Cairo. I was grading papers. I considered moving elsewhere. But the steady stream of his former students, mostly female, several of them also my students, began to intrigue me. One, Manal, sat with him for some time, talking earnestly, but not looking at him. She watched me. I smiled once or twice, but she did not seem to see me—she was looking through me, a very unsettling feeling. She was tall, thin, flat-chested, had an intense wide-eyed stare, which made her not attractive, but compelling, hard not to watch. Her most attractive feature was her hair, wild, black, huge, soft-looking. She wore unmatched clothing, plaids and polka dots, in colors that jarred, the pants too short for her long frame. I confess I am deeply smitten by her. She was telling Charles about an intimate problem but in a voice loud enough for anyone within twenty feet to hear. Manal is Palestinian. She said she drank whiskey and danced with boys, but that did not mean she slept with them.

One boy, who was an escort to a party in the desert, cornered her between two parked cars and tried to kiss her. She said no, fought, screamed. He said she'd done it before with other boys, she knew she had, everyone talked about it. His female Egyptian friends picked up on the refrain, when they were alone with Manal later, thinking they were preaching proper behavior but unknowingly playing into the boy's hands. He spread the rumor that she slept with someone to devalue Manal's reputation, in order to convince her she had nothing to lose if she slept with him. When she was finished with her story, Charles took her hand in both his hands. He said, 'Sleep with him. Egyptians despise Palestinians. What *have* you got to lose since you've already lost your reputation. Then, afterwards, you can spread the rumor that he could not keep an erection; that he confessed he loves men.' Manal was silent. Abruptly she laughed. 'You are funny, Dr. Charles. I almost believed you.'"

Ruqayyah has come onto the balcony during Ib's story about Charles. When Ib finishes, Charles does not respond. Ib knows Charles does not like being the subject of conversation. Ruqayyah asks if she can tell a story. Gamal says, "Do we have a choice?" Ruqayyah sucks in her breath.

"The last time I saw Annahíd before her . . . accident was a week ago," Ruqayyah says. "As always, Safeyya was gone. My sister does not interfere with my visits, but she prefers to be away. Gamal usually serves me coffee and Safeyya's excellent *molokhia*, and eating the soup makes me feel at least partly in the presence of my sister. Annahíd and I play. We work on her Legos—she's a builder like her grandfather and nearly as stubborn in her notions of form and beauty. We collaborate on monoprints with her mother's monotype press. I usually leave her to finish and clean up, which she always did— does—so uncomplainingly it breaks my heart. I suppose the reason I visit so regularly is to argue with Gamal. I love the fights. They are probably the same fights he and my sister have: about the Egyptianness of his daughter, about schooling, about Arabic and Islam. Except I know for a fact that Gamal defends Islam against Safeyya's attacks, just to irritate her. Last week we had a particularly confusing disagreement over the nature of Arabic—if it was God's tongue, Gamal asserted, how could it continue to evolve and why the necessity of policing classical Arabic—creating words from the old root words for new technology to avoid loanwords from other languages? I never got around to responding, be- cause we saw Annahíd in the doorway, holding our monoprint, staring at the floor. She said something like, 'Aunt Samar'—my old Christian name—'if I am so happy, why is everyone who talks about me so sad?'"

Gamal says to Ib, "Write this down." He tells another story, an obscure response to Ruqayyah's story.

"Gamal," Amina called from her chair on the deck over the foul-smelling Mediterranean. "Do be a dear and fetch some whiskey and club soda from the grocers on Falaki Street." Gamal finished translating a sentence from the Qur'an into understandable Arabic for Amina's son Mohammad—an Armenian Christian teaching a Moslem boy how to read his own bible. Then Gamal stood up gingerly, favoring a back injured by the sea that tried to suck him away from this horrid country, and he walked with wounded dignity out to the deck. *"S'il vous plaît, chère Madame Amina,"* he said quietly. "My name is Gamal-Leon, I am eighteen years old to-morrow, and I am not your servant." Amina fluttered and rose half out of her chaise longue. Then she floated gracefully back to earth, adjusting the bikini top that still looked good on her forty-three-year-old torso. "Dear dear me, young man, if you were my servant I'd have given you money and whispered the order in your handsome ear." Gamal-Leon blushed and took the ten-pound note Amina's mousy brother handed him. He left the house, shoulders stooped, and passed a garden bower where Amina's oldest child Aida was praying, in full headdress, with her two high school girlfriends, newly religious and ecstatically beautiful in their piety. In English Gamal said to Aida, "Each morning after you leave them, I worship the bedsheets your brown body wrinkles." Aida smiled benevolently at the unbeliever. "You know I don't understand a word of that sinful language," she replied, in the best BBC English money could buy.

▲ ▼ ▲ ▼ ▲ ▼ ▲ ▼ ▲ ▼ ▲

Gamal-Leon and Ib sit on the stone ledge at the end of Abul'ela Bridge near the Marriott Hotel. They are killing time until the car arrives to take them to the prison. The Nile slides by underneath. Thousands are out strolling in the dark, many back and forth across this homely bridge. The new 26th of July Street bridge has nudged this relic into relative disuse. The concrete flyover traverses the river south of and partly on top of the old fil-

143

igreed iron bridge, a typically Egyptian compromise with history. It now serves pedestrian and donkey cart traffic, shopkeepers, servants, and maids going to Zamalek's wealthy Egyptian and European population. A handful of people have gathered near them. They begin to shout and whistle. Gamal and Ib turn to look. An enormous floating island of weeds drifts toward the piling they are sitting on. The High Dam at Aswan has something to do with these river plants, the sign of an unhealthy ecosystem, a traffic-clotting parasite the annual flood used to keep in check. A man stands on this island. His feet are underwater, but the spongy fabric of the plants somehow keeps him afloat. His island is going upstream, against the current. It bumps into the piling and lodges there. He shouts up for help. The next minute Ib and Gamal take off their shoes, tie the laces, and sling the shoes over their shoulders. The man on the island watches this dainty procedure without comment. Ib and Gamal take as much of the plant material into their arms as they can. They push, but this only bunches up the island, at first not appearing to move the mass at all. But soon a cheer ripples down from the bridge. They *are* moving the thing. Gamal steps on to the living island and extends a hand to Ib. Together, on the edge of the thing, they sink to their knees, then to their waists, in the oily, crud-filled water. Ib thinks of the waterborne parasite that carries the disease bilharzia. The island's caretaker waves them toward him. The island is still moving, very slowly, out of the bridge piling's way. Each step they take toward the middle creates a lake and mounting panic in their movements. Voices from overhead shout encouragement. Spread your legs. Point your toes out like camels. Wave your arms in small circles. Gamal translates. The advice is good. They learn to walk on water. The buoyant plants underfoot feel like kelp. The current seems to gather the plants around their weight, so the faster they move the easier it is to stand upright. Just before they pass under the bridge, they are confident enough to look up for more than an instant. Their fans wave and cheer and shower them with flower petals collected from the ground under nearby flame trees. The petals bounce off their heads and arms, rubbery orange half-moons. Several people on the bridge have adopted Ib and Gamal's fashion and wear shoes, laces tied, around the neck. When they are under the bridge, the mystery of their movement against the current is solved: a small motorboat is dragging them. In open river, the island stretches out, and this makes standing on its surface thrillingly natural. Cairo has never seemed so magical, city lights reflecting off the water as they float along.

▲ ▼ ▲ ▼ ▲ ▼ ▲ ▼ ▲ ▼ ▲

The driver takes them up a narrow street in the old city, long past midnight. The city is still wide awake. Gamal and the driver have been arguing with great pleasure about Egyptian drivers. Gamal insists they are no better or worse than they have ever been; there are just hundreds of thousands more of them. The driver believes their godless, reckless behavior is symbolic of the breakdown in Egyptian society (or this is Ib's rough translation). The driver argues his point all the while driving at top speed, weaving in and out of traffic, slamming on his brakes or accelerating madly, shouting out the window joyfully "Your mother's vulva" in Arabic at men, women, children. Down the way a bit is a perfume merchant Ib frequents, mostly for conversation and history lessons—his grandfather opened the shop in 1887. The driver stops abruptly, as if he's lost his way. He turns to shake hands with his now good friend Gamal. "Is this the prison?" Gamal says. The driver smiles and shrugs his shoulders.

Ib and Gamal get out. The Peugeot chugs off. There is an old wooden door with a brass knocker in the shape of two praying hands, not a Muslim image. The door is to a three-story medieval building unmarked except for one *mashrabiyya* window high above and directly over the entrance. This cannot be the high-security prison that houses one of Sadat's assassins, Ib says. Gamal shakes his head, also puzzled. His shoulders slump and his head lolls forward in thought. He knocks. As he is knocking, the door opens. Inside is a large dark stone-floored entry hall similar to that of a mosque, tall-ceilinged but narrow, angled away from the interior space to make access to the paradise inside symbolically difficult. Several thick candles flicker wildly on the floor. The door is closed and the flames calm. A man stands behind a table at the far end of the hall waving vigorously for them to join him. He wears a black Malcolm X baseball cap and a white and blue pin-striped galabiya. Neither his clothing nor his behavior is that of a government official. Gamal seems to think the same thing, but he is playing along with the man, who introduces himself as the secretary to the warden. He tells Gamal, "You are *say-e-ab*," which means 'able to talk comfortably with a street sweeper or with the President of the country,' a skill Egyptians value but rarely find in the upper classes. Gamal dislikes being lumped with the upper classes, and Ib is surprised he does not dispute this observation hotly, more proof that he is as baffled by this performance as Ib is and that this is not another of Gamal's improvisations, or if it is he has lost control of it.

The secretary repeats the punch line of a joke Gamal told on the way here. Gamal looks at Ib, eyes big with amazement. The secretary laughs quietly, but he also has a cough, which competes with and eventually wins out over the laughter. Ib wonders for a moment how the joke was transmitted to the secretary—a listening device in the car? But Ib remembers they were stopped in a traffic jam beside a group of *menadis,* carwatchers, who were sitting on the hood of a diplomat's Mercedes near the British Embassy. The *menadis* enjoyed Gamal's joke as if it had been told in their living room. The *menadis* are part of the city-eye system, nothing so sinister as it seems at first to Westerners, just men desperate for work. The secretary takes a sip of tea. He orders more tea for his guests. He fills out several forms. He has Gamal sign each one, in quintuplicate. Despite the warmth he shows Gamal, he reads his passport word for word. He glances at Ib's and tosses it on the table.

He hands Gamal's passport to a runner, who has brought in more tea and forms. Suddenly it occurs to Ib, and he can't help saying out loud, "If this is a prison, where are the machine guns? Where are the armed guards?"

⁂

The prisoner speaks: "An American expert on artificial intelligence says the most common argument against the possibility of human thought in computers is that they have no souls. Then he asks the next logical question: But can a soul learn as a computer can? This American humanist thinks he's being clever, but the Sufis have known for centuries that souls do learn." Because the guard is watching, Ib writes this down. He could pretend to write. He is so very tired, the idea of not transcribing what this prisoner says is seductive, physically appealing, the way a hot bath would be, or making love very slowly to Gamal's sister-in-law. But he writes the thought down. "Look at me and you look at our sheikh," the prisoner says. "It's not that we appear to be the same, we don't look alike. My skin is coffee-colored. They shave my head every month and my beard every week. But we share the same soul right now." Ib transcribes this, not frantically, not hurrying to keep up with the prisoner. Ib writes confident that he is putting down the exact words of the prisoner. This is completely unlike the experience of scribbling down Gamal-Leon's stories this evening, which was more like translation, remembering dreams. Ib's sudden talent for dictation is not surprising—he has been practicing all night, and there may be something about the prisoner's voice and almost musical delivery, as opposed to Gamal's manic style, which accounts for Ib's newfound facility. The prisoner says, "You will recall my words easily, Ib, because they are ethereal, made of light." Ib is too sleepy to remember if he spoke aloud what he thought he was thinking. He decides not to be spooked by this man.

Ib puts his pen down. "How do you know my name? We were not introduced. And the secretary barely looked at my passport. What kind of place is this?" Gamal is sitting on the small bed, cleaning his nails with a penknife. A penknife in a prison.

"Don't let this guy fool you, Ib," Gamal says. "He does it all with smoke and mirrors. I knew him before he got religion. He was a good actor then, too. The roles he played best were the holy men, the sincere repentant sinners. The best acting he ever did was Alyosha in a performance of *The Brothers K* we put on at the Actors' Theater. But he was a rake and a *hashhash* off stage, smoking hashish even in his sleep. Women learned never to be alone with him. One young girl sprayed him with Mace. We were all very proud of her, even our Alyosha here, who joined in the congratulations as if he had not been the cause of her heroism. It wasn't that he was unrepentant, he was unaware he'd done anything wrong. Until he met his Sufis."

The prisoner laughs at the memories. He reaches across the bed and squeezes Gamal's chin affectionately. He makes a kissing noise, but Ib, for the moment, is rereading the prisoner's words, and when Ib looks up he sees only the trace of puckered lips, evidence of the briefest flicker of irony on the prisoner's face, of a sarcastic kiss.

"No," the prisoner says. "It was a divine kiss."

Gamal falls with a thud against the wall, saying, "Give me a break." The guard jolts awake. He sees Gamal's penknife. He wants to say something about it—Ib reads

151

this on the guard's face. Then the prisoner winks at the guard, and the guard's body relaxes in his chair behind the bars. He drifts off to sleep again. He's snoring soon. "Would you quit it with the Obi-Wan Kenobi business," Gamal says to the prisoner.

"So how do you know my name?" Ib asks. The prisoner glances at Ib, as if at something on Ib's face, a smudge or piece of lint, but not at Ib himself. Then he's animated by another set of thoughts entirely and he turns to Gamal. He speaks to him in Arabic. Until now they have spoken English. Gamal answers curtly, not wanting to be drawn in. Another guttural rain of back-of-the-throat fricatives from the prisoner. He is talking theology, and in Arabic he sounds very sad; the years in prison, the beatings, and the deprivation show on him. Ib can make out some of what he is saying. Gamal's daughter's name is mentioned a few times and Gamal bristles. The prisoner calms him. But Ib is too tired to translate. He has to listen to Arabic twice in his mind— once in the original, then again in broken English. It is a relief not to have to listen, but the stone floor and coarse brick wall soon become uncomfortable, and Ib begins to feel left out. They are being rude to him. A large cockroach skitters across the floor under the guard. Ib looks glumly down at the few sentences he wrote of the prisoner's bizarre thoughts. He thinks—or perhaps he says aloud, "Stop it. I'm supposed to be taking notes. I can't do Arabic at this hour of the night. Speak English."

The prisoner stands up and walks toward Ib. He reaches out with his good hand—the other is atrophied—and Ib flinches. The prisoner's response to this, the look in his eyes, is surprisingly hurt. Ib grabs the good hand as it is retreating and jumps up, making it look as if the prisoner has helped him to his feet. The prisoner guides Ib over to the bed. "Sit," he says. "I'll stand. I'll pace. I need to walk every few minutes or I lose my mind. How long have I been a prisoner, Gamal?" Gamal holds up four lazy fingers twice.

They are quiet. The prisoner paces. Ib wants to write down a physical description of the prisoner, but he can't. He remembers how a friend who nearly converted to Islam described his first encounter with a powerful and respected sheikh, for whom the usually low-key and skeptical Englishman could find no other word but beautiful. The Englishman said the sheikh's face seemed to radiate an inner light.

▲ ▼ ▲ ▼ ▲ ▼ ▲ ▼ ▲ ▼ ▲

The prisoner and Gamal are playing chess. The guard is gone. There has been a long silence since the last faint click of a move. The room is stark, with nothing—no books or pictures on the walls—other than the bed, a chamber pot, and the chess set with pharaonic pieces. The prisoner says, "Chess problems demand the same virtues that characterize all worthwhile art: originality, invention, conciseness, harmony, complexity, and splendid insincerity."

Ib tells the prisoner that he has read that somewhere. The prisoner's eyes gleam. Gamal says with a sigh, "Nabokov. We did a play about him."

The prisoner makes a move and Gamal groans. The prisoner stands and yawns and goes over to his small, barred, permanently open window. Ib follows him. The sun is an hour or two from rising. Beside a minaret is the symbol of Islam: the waning crescent moon and its companion star.

"Do you observe Ramadan?" Ib asks. "I mean, do they allow you to observe it in here?" Ib answers for the prisoner, "A stupid question. How can they not allow you to observe the fast?" The prisoner looks out on the ruins of another medieval building. "What was it?" Ib asks. "A hospital," the prisoner says. "When Europe was squatting around rude fires in a dark age, we had sophisticated medicine, hospital poets, elaborate indoor plumbing."

Ib asks again how the prisoner knew his name.

The prisoner sits down on the floor beneath this window and beckons Ib. Ib sits beside him on the cool stones. The prisoner says, "We know many things. We can see into the hearts of men. My friends on the outside have done some research on you. We were curious. I have heard your name mentioned before. The translations of Rumi you did are very good for an unbeliever, almost convincing."

Ib says, "You are in a high-security prison. I assume the government is not going to allow you open access to your friends. How did you get your information?"

"Let us just say that I have knowledge. Do you know the Arabic word *batin?*" Ib nods. *Batin* is knowledge of God in the world—knowledge hidden from ordinary men. "Claiming to have it is the same as not having it,

155

so I won't claim to have *batin*." He giggles, a boyish and naive sound, yet this man sounds more complex, sophisticated, tragic by the minute. "But I learn many things. For example, your father died a few days ago."

"My stepfather," Ib says, his skin tightening.

"What is that word, Gamal?" the prisoner asks. Gamal says the word in Arabic. "Ah. But you loved him very much. You learned your life from him, you grew under his care." Ib notices Gamal is shivering. "There is also the matter of an Egyptian woman you think you got into trouble. You were mistaken, she is recovering well from a small surgery. You misconceived something someone said about her at the Dar al-Kutub, a natural misunderstanding. But you were wrong to flirt with her, and you know you were flirting with her. You were wrong not for cultural or moral reasons. You hurt her feelings. Do you understand that?"

Stunned and chastened, Ib lowers his head and mumbles, "Yes, sir. I understand." Sir? What is going on here? Why is Gamal smoothing out the blanket around the chessboard? Where is his irony when Ib needs it?

But Ib finds himself liking this man, the prisoner, against every rational fiber in his body. The prisoner is smiling and saying, "You met a few of my friends tonight. I am sorry you did not join them for *iftar*. But I believe you made the right choice, following Gamal. Gamal is not an easy man to like, but once you do, you'll find it is hard to dislike him as much as you want to."

Gamal says, "Another story," miming for Ib the act of writing. Ib already has pen in hand and notebook open.

Report from el-Hussein Hospital, 1009 A.H.

The day before Ramadan soldiers brought us the unbeliever in chains, but he seems to have been forgotten, so I ordered the chains cut. The European moved delicately for a few days, as if still weighed down by the heavy anklets. He was found wandering the desert near Sakkara, blind from staring into the sun, lips black from drinking his own urine. He did not speak the one true language, praise be on His tongue, so no one understands the poor middle-aged man. He showed no soul except when the hospital musicians played for the wounded soldiers nearby; then he looked animated by some cruel memory of a wife's deception or a son's disobedience. The hospital storyteller sang a poem about a Christian holy man who drank from stone, but the European did not notice he was being sung to. Stung, the storyteller generalized: "Nazarenes know nothing about their faith." My first wife refused to open her doors to him. My second agreed without a word on the subject from me. That night at home I found him making beautiful woman-shaped boxes with my carpentry tools. The next night we rode to the Christian prostitution district. The sound of so much naked flesh made tears pop from his blind eyes, but he refused to go upstairs with anyone. Instead, he sang, a sound like a trapped animal gnawing off its foot.

▲ ▼ ▲ ▼ ▲ ▼ ▲ ▼ ▲ ▼ ▲

Gamal wins the chess game. After a moment Gamal tells the prisoner there are two nearly identical Armenian phrases, *shod guh shirem* and *shod guh sirem*. The first means "I urinate very much"; the second, "I like very much." Once, he stayed up all night to finish a review of a play for *Rose al-Yusuf* magazine—and the review triggered a feverish revision of more than half of his own play, written several years before and which he had not looked at in two years—and the next morning, he gave a talk at the Armenian Church in Abbasiya on an Armenian writer in Russia. All through the talk he kept saying *shod guh shirem,* instead of *shod guh sirem.* There were over a hundred bodies in the audience, a great crowd for a lecture in Armenian. Not one person snickered. Not one person corrected him. Afterwards, the old bookbinder Kyril Hamalian approached him and greeted him warmly. He praised many aspects of Gamal's talk. He criticized one or two interpretations of the writer's weakest novel. Then he said, almost as an aside, as if it were not at all important but for Gamal's private storehouse of information only, that he had misspoken *shod guh sirem.* "It's nothing really. An elementary error. We all make these mistakes. We speak Arabic, French, English, German, Italian. How can we be expected to keep all the words, let alone the pronunciations, straight?"

Gamal ran to the tram and jumped on just as it was leaving the platform. He read through the notes for his talk. He had not only mispronounced the word, he'd misspelled it in the text, which he'd written, clear-headed and well-rested, days before the talk. In speaking such a phrase, one might stumble and misstate oneself.

"But in writing, the act became much more sinister, a much graver sin against the language I dream in. For a few hours, I despised Arabic," Gamal says. "I took my play and burnt what I thought was the only copy of it, page by page. My wife discovered me just as the last page curled up in flames. She left the room and returned a moment later with the copy I'd been rewriting the night before. She had been folding laundry in my room and found the new version. She'd read it and even written a few comments on it—tough and helpful criticism. I had completely forgotten about the revised draft. Here I was so smugly burning one copy of the play while my devious multilingual mind had stored away—or hidden—the fact that there was another copy, a freshly revised edition that I'd been working on the night before. My wife did not say a word. She could read into the moment that it was just another irrational outburst against my unnatural mother tongue, Arabic, which would make Safeyya sad if she heard me speak it at full volume—or even in a whisper."

The prisoner says, "I could say Arabic is so beautiful because it was the last language Allah chose to speak to us in. But you'll have a tantrum, and my logic is wrong, anyway. Each tongue is Allah's tongue. He hears every language known to man. Your Armenian mind is jealous of Arabic and your Arabic mind makes fun of Armenian. I see how disconcerting this is to you. But listen to the message your soul is sending you. Study Armenian again. Arabic won't care. Armenian is a lovely language, uncorrupted by other tongues, as Hebrew was. There are some disadvantages to knowing several languages equally well, but there are benefits, too. What does Rushdie say, something is always gained in the translation, as well as being lost?"

Ib is impressed by this little speech of the prisoner's—and by a jailed fundamentalist's reference to Salman Rushdie.

"Get the hell out of my mind," Gamal says. "You're just acting. Without a script, you wouldn't have a clue. I remember when you first began to memorize the Qur'an. It was the same as learning your lines for a play. And you had no trouble pretending sincerity. It always came naturally. I hope Mubarak throws away the key to your cell."

The prisoner says, "I love you, too." But the look of emotional exhaustion on his face is more than Ib can bear to watch.

"Damn it," Gamal says. "Now he's quoting Edward G. Robinson in *Double Indemnity.*"

"No," the prisoner says. "It's Fred MacMurray."

"Whatever. But I must know something before I leave," Gamal says. He is pacing the small room. Ib and the prisoner occupy the bed, and the room feels to Ib bizarrely like a college dorm room. "I need to know what is hidden, I want to know what you see. Can you see guilt in me? Have I committed some terrible crime?"

The prisoner says, "I know you well, my friend, but in the wrong context. You are not of my tariqa, you're not even Muslim. We knew each other long ago, we were both different men."

Gamal says, "I've already written this interview, I wrote it a week ago. But I can change what I wrote. I'll say

162

that you're a fraud. That you cannot see under the surface of reality, beyond the body and the mind."

The prisoner rubs one hand over his stubble. He does not seem disturbed by this threat. Ib says to Gamal, "Surely you know why Annahíd ate the plant. Do you need this mystical mumbo jumbo to tell you something you already know?"

The prisoner says, "The great Iranian revolutionary philosopher Ali Shari'ati says man is always in motion. He is a choice, a struggle, a constant becoming. He is an infinite migration within himself, from clay to God."

"Guard! *Ya rais!*" Gamal yells. "Let's go, Ib. I've had enough of this crap. *Vas-y,* go, go."

The guard arrives, opens the door. Gamal strides off. Ib hesitates. The prisoner ignores him. He is lost in thought. Ib has the momentary urge to ask the prisoner's permission to woo his ex-wife, Ruqayyah, but luckily he cannot form the physical words around the idiotic request. Instead, he whispers, so Gamal won't hear him, "Thank you." The prisoner looks up. The guard closes the door and roughly pushes Ib to get

163

moving. The prisoner shows no emotion on his face, but he says quietly, "Don't underestimate us, Ib. Don't thank us. We are much stronger than you know."

The guard shoves so hard, Ib falls on the dirt floor. The guard kicks Ib with a slippered foot, which should not hurt as much as it does.

▲ ▼ ▲ ▼ ▲ ▼ ▲ ▼ ▲ ▼ ▲

Outside, limping, Ib has trouble catching up with Gamal, who sprints up and down alleys, looking for something. He finds what he's searching for finally on a cul-de-sac off Darb as-Saada, a beautifully maintained 1940s Chevrolet that has a fine shroud of dust covering it. Gamal opens the unlocked driver's door, pulls out his keys, says, "Get in. You drive. We're going to Safeyya's house at Sakkara."

Ib has never driven a car in Cairo. Gamal is asleep and snoring loudly the moment he's seated. Ib tests the horn, an essential tool of motoring in Egypt. Gamal snorts but remains unconscious. Even in sleep, Gamal sounds actorish, false. Ib takes a few moments to get a feel for the high clutch, the large steering wheel, the straight, stiff seats.

He is preternaturally alert. He has never felt so awake. Half an hour ago he never felt so weary. The car starts with a very pleasing low rumble.

Driving through the now empty old city is a joy. He avoids the easy exits from the maze and finds himself motoring down some of the same streets twice. What's the rush? An hour earlier the city was bustling. Now it is quiet. Ib passes three people along the way on his tour of medieval Cairo: a flour-coated baker riding his bicycle with a pallet piled high with 'aish baladi—dirt-flavored peasant bread—balanced on his head (the boy waved testily for Ib to overtake him, but Ib perversely stayed behind him for a few hundred yards, marveling at his grace); also two bearded young men in spotless white galabiyas and lace skullcaps—members of the Muslim Brotherhood—working on the engine of a small truck under the only streetlight in the neighborhood. These men remind Ib of the prisoner, a figure so implausible he has begun to dissolve from Ib's memory just moments after leaving him.

Later, as if making its own decision, the Chevrolet veers onto a flyover that takes them out of the old city. Ib accepts the accident of departure, enjoys glimpsing in apartment windows at families still awake, playing games, smoking *shisha* pipes, singing. Then they rise above even the highest buildings.

These flyovers, efficient and depressing modernist additions to the city, connect different parts of Cairo in a brutal European idea of progress. Pedestrians never use the flyovers. Even Egyptians consider them too dangerous. But here, a long way off, is a man on foot carrying a briefcase. Ib flashes the high beams at this poor fellow (an Egyptian would be driving without lights and in this instance would turn them on, blinding the pathetic walker). The pedestrian lurches and falls on the railing of the four-story-high flyover, then rights himself just as Ib is passing him. The pedestrian shouts in English, "Your daughter will marry an unbeliever!" It's Charles Mattimore. Ib brakes and Gamal rolls forward against the door but does not surface from his twitchy dreams. When Ib steps out of the car, Charles takes flight. Ib laughs and calls to him. Charles translates his awkward scamper into a dignified pirouette and walks slowly back to the vehicle.

Charles is nevertheless breathing heavily when he settles into the back seat, and he asks for a moment to compose himself. He does so partly by pulling out a lovely silver flask, which could only have whiskey in it. They pass a broken-down taxi a few hundred yards ahead. The driver is sitting on the hood and waves forlornly. "Don't stop," Charles whispers. Charles sips from his flask, then replaces the cap. "I would offer you some, but I know your religion prohibits alcohol."

Ib smiles and says, "Is it bourbon or Scotch?" He knows the very thought of bourbon makes Charles' blood boil. Charles stares at the flask for a long time before handing it to Ib. "I don't expect you'll know the difference between a twelve-year-old and an eighteen-year-old whiskey," he says. "Enjoy it anyhow."

"Well," Charles says. "That's the last time I allow a Palestinian to give me a guided tour of Cairo. He claimed he was Sudanese, but I saw through that lie. It is rather unhealthy to admit to that heritage here, just as a Jew wouldn't advertise his Hebrew past in London. I don't know why, but as a favor to the fellow, I said I would go with him to the City of the Dead, where his family lives." The City of the Dead is the huge cemetery out-

167

side Cairo now inhabited by hundreds of thousands of migrants from the countryside. "I was gambling, I suppose, on finding he has a sister as pretty as he was," Charles says. "At three in the morning?" Ib asks. "These Mohammedans," Charles says. "They don't sleep, you know. And this fellow had never driven into the old city despite living adjacent to it these many years. Got us hopelessly lost. Only found the flyover by sheerest luck. I had finally convinced him to take me home, when the car let out a death rattle and died. He insisted on staying with the thing until dawn, so he could see to repairs. No reasoning with him."

"Why would you accept the invitation in the first place? Where has this sympathy for the Palestinians come from?" Ib asks, although he knows the answer. "I didn't realize you had the slightest interest in Islamic architecture."

"Never actually been to the City of the Dead," Charles says. "Leaving day after tomorrow. Mightn't ever come back to Cairo—hope I never do anyway."

Ib drives on. He takes the last warm swallow of Scotch. Charles pulls a book out of his briefcase and begins to read. Ib turns on the dim overhead light for him. The drive is very easy so late at night, except for the occasional double-trailer trucks going ninety miles an hour in the wrong lane and the half-dozen police barricades. But even the military police offer fresh pleasures, new ways of ingratiating himself, amusing diversions, and Ib feels sympathy for these men, who are only doing what they can to combat the radical fundamentalists.

Of all people, Charles is passionately pro-Palestinian. "Israel," Charles says, looking up from his book, which Ib notes is by an American Jewish convert to Islam, Abdullah Schleifer's *The Fall of Jerusalem.* Schleifer is a colleague at the American University who lived in Jerusalem during the 1967 War. Charles and Schleifer despise one another. "Israel," Charles repeats. "A charming country run by ruthlessly efficient people. But what about the old Palestinian villages? Don't you imagine the Israelis would want to eradicate the one geographical memory they're daily confronted by? They razed hundreds of hilltop villages in the years after forty-eight. The Palestinians, for centuries, had used prickly pear cactus plants to mark off boundaries of farmland. Especially around the villages, the prickly pear was ever-present. Problem is, you can't eradicate this cactus

169

as easily as you can the Palestinian people. Always grows back. Dig down five feet and it still comes back. Perhaps this is why the Israelis call their own native-born citizens 'sabras,' which means the prickly pear itself. Even from the air you can see the ghostly outlines of the old towns. Why do the Israelis leave these guilty plants? I should think with all their other technological achievements, they'd surely have found a way to eliminate the prickly pear cactus. I imagine they need to be reminded daily of the tenacity of the Palestinian people. But perhaps the idea is to taunt the few remaining Palestinians in Israel proper with the memory of their old homes."

Charles fell in love with a Palestinian male student's older sister, who would have nothing to do with Charles. In an effort to win the sister, Charles wrote letter after letter to a professor of economics he knew at the University of Wisconsin to get the girl's brother a scholarship there. The boy was accepted and given full tuition and stipend into the graduate program, but the sister married a forty-five-year-old businessman in Oman on the eve of the boy's departure. Charles completely neglected his job at the American University, which was the official reason given for his firing. But there is the possibility that the girl's father, a major donor to the university, ordered him fired. Ib knows this story from several sources (none Charles) and trusts only the essence of it, not the particulars, but he is curious to hear direct evidence of Charles' passionate and contrary sympathy for the Palestinians.

Ib stays on the main southern highway along the Nile until they come to a narrow wooden bridge off to the right, which he turns onto without thinking. They pass through a tiny village and make a detour around several cows in the road, which takes them down a dirt road for a mile in a field of wheat the U.S. has been buying from and giving back to Egypt since the Camp David accords. They meet up with another main road and Ib turns right.

A sign for Sakkara pointing off onto a perpendicular road becomes visible from behind a bush just as they pass it. Ib stops the car, backs up, and turns onto the road, although he has no idea if this is indeed the way to Gamal's country home. But he does not want to wake his passenger. Nor does Charles show the slightest interest in their journey. They pass through a lovely palm forest, the ground rounded in small pregnant hills between barren valleys. The crescent moon shines through the trees like a searchlight.

They come to another fork in the road. "Which way?" Ib asks Charles, who replies, "Do what Sadat did when he went out for a ride with Nasser's chauffeur shortly after Nasser died. The chauffeur signaled left but turned right." Ib laughs and obeys. Within a hundred yards they arrive at the gates of a multi-domed pseudo-peasant-style house at the edge of the desert. A man is standing by the trellis entryway. Ib leans out his window. "You are Ramzi?" he asks. The man nods and points with a half-eaten chicken leg up the driveway.

Gamal wakes with a start. He looks around. He smiles. "Good work. I knew I could guide you in my dreams. Very excellent driving."

Charles says, "Preposterous. I've been here a dozen times. If Ib had made a wrong turn, rest assured I'd have told him so." Gamal exhibits no surprise that Charles is a passenger. Everything that can happen does happen in Egypt.

Gamal jumps out of the car. He dances along the gravel driveway beside the Chevrolet. He skips to the spot he wants Ib to park in and jumps up and down. Despite Charles' logical and Gamal's lyrical explanation of how he got them here, Ib prefers to think that the vehicle itself knew the way.

There are three other cars parked in the circular driveway. The front door of the house opens and Ruqayyah strides efficiently out toward them, a finger to her lips. "Quiet. The poor little thing only just fell asleep. Let's take *suhour* out in the desert, away from the house." *Suhour* is the light meal before sunrise, the last before the day of fasting. "You boys bring the folding chairs and tables from around the pool."

▲ ▼ ▲ ▼ ▲ ▼ ▲ ▼ ▲ ▼ ▲

A lull in the conversation. A warm breeze wafts over the small sandy hill carrying the smell of the Red Sea, which is a hundred miles away. Ruqayyah draws Ib's name in the sand again and again, except she spells it "Ebb." Ruqayyah has not asked a single question about the prison visit. Perhaps only Ib hears a door slam in the house some distance away, so he is expecting someone to emerge from the trellised walkway. After a moment, when no figure has come out, Ib turns his attention again to Ruqayyah's lovely fingers. But on the periphery of his vision, he sees a small, oddly illuminated body appear on the grass by the pool. The person skirts the riding ring and heads straight for this group. Slowly he understands why the figure looks so brightly lit. The little girl is completely naked. She walks with very adult steps closer and closer to the edge of the desert. Ib feels an illogical wave of lust for this child. He does not want the others to see her yet, so he pretends not to notice her. But as milliseconds pass and no one does see Annahíd moving ever nearer, Ib begins to hate himself. Still, he cannot bring himself to announce, "Well, here comes Little Miss Sunshine herself." Charles will realize he's been staring at this vision and saying nothing. When she hits the sand, she does a mincing but also vaguely martial dance across the dozen or so yards, which Ib decides is the way she walks on this sand when it is so hot she can't walk on it, and at the same moment he concludes and speaks aloud, "She's sleepwalking!"

▲ ▼ ▲ ▼ ▲ ▼ ▲ ▼ ▲ ▼ ▲

"Are you Ib?" Annahíd asks. The girl's voice is husky and disturbingly grown up. The reason for her hoarseness, Ib heard earlier, is that her stomach was pumped and a tube forced down her throat. He answers that he is indeed Ib. She wiggles restlessly under her blanket and briefly disappears. She reappears and laughs, a sexy laugh. "That's a funny name," she says. "I dreamed of it first, then Mother told me you might be at the house and I just couldn't imagine anyone would be named Ib." Ib says he'll change it if she wants. "No, no, don't you dare. You know it is very bad to change your name. I like Ib. It starts and then it stops. It sounds like something a mouse would say. Don't you think so, Baba?" Gamal-Leon is startled and he says nothing. The group has formed a circle on their blankets around the little child, who has, without any ado, fallen into a deep luxurious sleep. Ruqayyah rocks a bit. Safeyya rubs her own forehead tenderly. The tahini, pickled carrots and cauliflower, and pans of oily cakes sit untouched on a low brass table. The empty lawn chairs surround them. Gamal-Leon crawls across to his daughter and pulls the blanket up over her shoulders. But just as abruptly as she fell asleep, she awakes and says to her father, "Tell me a story, Daddy."

Gamal starts in without pause, "The day you were born I had to be at the dress rehearsal for *A Flea in Her Ear.* The director, an American woman who'd lived in Sweden for ten years, pulled me off the stage by my false beard when she learned that my wife was in labor. 'Get out of here, Gamal. This silly old farce isn't worth missing the birth of your daughter.' She did not know you'd be a girl; this was simply her American/Swedish feminism filling in the blank with a generic female. Two actors and a technician, all Egyptian men, overheard the director's remark, which sparked a controversy that lasted many hours. You landed safely, and your mother and I sat for who knows how long just watching you breathe. When I returned to the theater, I found the whole group of actors and technicians sitting in a circle on the stage holding hands, chanting quietly. The director looked up at me with tears in her eyes. 'If I offended you by predicting that your child would be a girl,' she said, 'I did not mean to. Your culture is wrong to despair at the birth of every female, but I may have been insensitive to your feelings and superstitions.' I stood above the circle for a moment. I wanted nothing more than to rehearse, to release the amazing energy your birth had filled me with. I wanted to make a large audience writhe with mirth. I desperately needed the electricity of a properly timed chain of words and action and gesture. I also felt the need to defend myself against the charges this American woman had made. In character and still in costume, I began the play, taking my largely stationary role around the circle of actors. They interacted woodenly with me at first, but eventually in response to my own inspired performance, they were brilliant. Fortunately, I am on stage every minute of the play. After a while, the actors stood and retreated to their positions, and the tech people disappeared into the rotating scenery, beds that turned on platforms. At one point, I reached down to lead the director by the hand off stage. She was the only person left of the circle. But when she saw my hands she screamed. I had not seen them either. They were black and blue, mostly black. Your mother had gripped them fiercely during labor. She kept saying to me, 'Don't let go,' as if I were the one holding on. You were a relatively easy birth, honey, but all mothers are like wild animals in labor. The circle formed again around my hands. The rehearsal ended. The actors were crying, the techies staring wide-eyed. Everyone wanted to touch my hands. The director could not control herself and began to sob. The men who'd given her a hard time wept, too, and everyone, except me, held hands."

Charles pulls a bottle of wine from his briefcase and ceremoniously uncorks it. He is clearly unhappy with the flawed bubbly glass of the dark blue water glasses, but Ib can see him physically deciding it is not worth the trouble to call for Ramzi to fetch wineglasses, a rare show of practicality. He pours wine for everyone, including Annahíd. Ruqayyah holds her glass away from her body. Annahíd cups her glass against her collarbone. Charles says, "Notwithstanding your father's peculiar sense of what is proper for a young girl's ears, may I propose a toast to you, young Annahíd?" Annahíd looks to her mother for an answer. Safeyya, who has gripped Gamal's stockinged foot, simply smiles at her daughter. "Annahíd," Charles says, "I want you to live a long life, preferably in one of the European capitals, with lots of books and art and admirers." Ib has been staring down at the sand, and when he looks up, there are tears in his eyes despite annoyance with Charles (and an unhappy suspicion that Charles and Ruqayyah have slept together). Annahíd has fallen asleep again, and her glass of wine has spilled into the desert, leaving a purple S on the sand. "Why are you here, Charles?" Ruqayyah asks. "Samar!" Safeyyah says. Charles says, "I can promise you I'll never set foot in this dismal country again, after tomorrow. Unless of

178

course I am asked to come back and paid in advance
for a lecture series on, say, the poetics of Lord Cromer's
prose." "Can't we do something about this creature,
Gamal?" Ruqayyah says. "Doesn't Father have some
bookkeeping Charles can do in the house?"

Charles, ignoring Ruqayyah, asks Ib shyly if he would
write down one of *his* stories. Ib does not reply, but
Gamal nods, as if releasing his servant.

The foreigners sit on the gold-trimmed couches as if
they own them. My master is hurt by their whispering.
The two men see my painted toenails and let their eyes
crawl up my legs like insects. In the kitchen I consult
Ali, who speaks their tongue. He says they want to understand a book they brought with them, which my
master wrote. If it takes three people to read a book, no
thank you, I am glad to be ignorant. They leave without
thanking my master in the language of the Prophet. I
wash the dishes and put away the liquor (my master
averted his glance when they drank) and scrub the floor
especially around where the foreigners sat. I change
into my best dress, tie on my scarf, and set out for home
across the river. One of the foreigners is waiting at the

179

other end of the bridge, neck bulging from the collar noosed around it, white fingers tapping a cane. He hands me three twenty-pound notes, more than my master pays me for two months of work. He pretends to speak our language and says he would be honored to have me work for him. I see the unspeakable lust in his eyes, worse than my husband after he takes the children to the zoo. But his weak hands and corpse's pallor and clothes that choke him make me pity his mother, who must bleed every morning she sees him.

▲ ▼ ▲ ▼ ▲ ▼ ▲ ▼ ▲ ▼ ▲

Sand. Camel tracks. A donkey braying. The wind has shifted and the awful odor of the neighboring chicken farm stings their nostrils. A cock crows absentmindedly. Annahíd snores like a teakettle seconds away from whistling. "An Egyptian child and she's allergic to dust!" Safeyya whispers. Charles Mattimore digs with the toy shovel Annahíd carried out to them. Charles never does anything without purpose, but he is clearly digging out a Gothic letter *H.* Ib massages Ruqayyah/Samar's neck. It was established by general consensus that Samar loved only European and American men, but Ruqayyah loves only born Muslims because she does not want to be the expert on Islam in her household. Safeyya took Ib's journal without asking and was reading the stories he wrote earlier in the evening. Now she is concentrating fiercely one moment and writing in the book the next with an amazing look of calm on her beautiful face. Annahíd wakes up and speaks: "Daddy. When we drove to the hospital I went outside the car for a few minutes. Yes I did. I was flying low over the car. Your hand was outside the window tapping on the roof of the car. I wanted to say, Stop that, but I couldn't talk. You took off your wedding ring. You did. You are always doing that, and you tried to put it on your pinky, but it flew off and bounced twice and then went high up in the air, and simple as pie I swooped down and caught the ring in my teeth. I did."

Ib watches Gamal feel his left ring finger and then his right: no wedding ring. Ib recalls the unsettling vision he had earlier in the evening of *X*, naked and dead on an operating table with a gold wedding band in her mouth. Now he remembers *X*'s name: Nermine. Annahíd, naked and growling playfully, crawls across the sand to her mother. Ib climbs painfully to his feet—his ribs aching where the guard kicked—and takes her little blanket over to mother and daughter. But Ramzi arrives at that moment from the house and whispers in Safeyya's ear. "Telephone?" she says. "Who would be calling at five in the morning?" She rises to go. Ib sits and Annahíd creeps onto his defenseless lap. Gamal asks his daughter, "Did you make this dream up? Did you really see my ring fly off the roof of the car? You must have seen it from the rear window." Annahíd digs her fingers into Ib's lap, close to his groin. She yawns up into Ib's face, and he smells ambergris. Annahíd is trying to burrow between his legs like a beetle through the crack of fingers in a closed fist. Annahíd says, "I did too fly over the car." She coughs. There is a long moment of silence. Charles says, "Is it obvious only to me that the child died briefly and left her body? She reentered her body to save your miserable marriage, Gamal." Safeyya returns carrying a cordless phone. "Ramzi does not believe the phone can leave the house, no matter how many times we explain," she says. "It's for you, Ib."

▲ ▼ ▲ ▼ ▲ ▼ ▲ ▼ ▲ ▼ ▲

"When shepherds become friends the sheep are lost," Gamal is saying to Ib's mother on the telephone.

Gamal-Leon listens intently for a moment. Annahíd has moved over to his lap. Gamal laughs with completely unfeigned pleasure. Ib's mother tells good stories. "I know, I know, yes," Gamal says. "He's not as slow-motion as he seems at first. No, don't worry. He's among friends here." Ib hears a splash in the distance. By the pool, under the cabana, Hanaa is holding a bathrobe over one arm and reading a book. Unseen below her George is probably swimming his early morning laps. Annahíd whispers to Ib, "Why is your mother calling from the United States? Isn't that awfully expensive? Is something wrong in your family?" Charles puts out his cigarette in the sand and blows a smoke ring for the girl, which she spears with her middle finger. Charles blinks, disconcerted by this accidental rude gesture from Annahíd, and he answers for Ib, shakily at first, "Americans don't know how to have a private conversation." "Isn't it true, though," says Ruqayyah from under a large sun hat— the sun is fifteen minutes from rising, the sky pinking— "that you yourself were born beneath a magnolia tree in Mobile, Alabama? I saw your passport once." Charles has trouble lighting his next cigarette, the fancy lighter gasping and spluttering. "You probably don't know why the medieval Islamic empire failed, Samar," Charles says evenly. "Christian Europe, rebuffed during the Cru-

183

sades, discovered another way to India, and the Middle
East lost its importance as a central trading route. All
the gold and silver the Spaniards found in the Americas
also had a disastrous effect on the acquired wealth of
the Muslim empire, because the value of the metals declined so much. The discovery of the Americas devas-
tated Islam, which has never forgotten the insult."
Gamal is saying, on the phone, "Ib and I have known
each other for three years. We both teach at the American University. We are working together on the translation of a play I wrote about an Egyptian troupe of
magicians and Sufi mystics who barnstorm the American Midwest in the 1870s. Yes, yes, he does. When Ib
fell in love with my sister-in-law he began to write the
play in exactly the language I imagined but could not
carry out myself in English. Her name is Samar, which
means 'evening conversation.' They will name their first
son Charles. Excuse me?" Gamal is silent. Everyone is
listening. "No, I am an actor and I write for a few newspapers. I teach theater. I do many things badly. Yes? He
is right here. It was lovely to speak with you." Gamal
hands the phone to Charles, who passes it on to Ib.
Safeyya says, "Gamal! It's a transatlantic call. Will you
never change?" Ib listens in the earpiece for the familiar

voice, the familiar noise of the kitchen, but all he hears is an ocean of static. "She's not there," Ib says. "Baba," Annahíd says sharply. Ib's maid took a message a week ago that there had been a death in his family. Apparently she had been asked to please not tell him this, but to have him call back immediately. There had been a half-hour wait for the operator at the American University to patch through his return call. It was a guilty relief to learn it was only his stepfather, but he was blindsided by grief an hour later.

"Write this down," Gamal says to Ib. "Gamal," Safeyya says. "Let him call his mother back. Do you know the code for the U.S., Ib? I know it." But Ib shakes his head and picks up his journal and uncaps his pen. Gamal's last story of the night:

From Annahíd's bedroom window you can see two minarets across the Nile, but on the near bank in a tin shack next to a large nursery men sit at night and chant the Qur'an and talk of God. Try to get Annahíd to sleep with that racket, well just imagine how hard it is. She will jump out of bed when I'm not looking, and I find her

leaning over the balcony railing, straining to hear them.
What are they saying? she asks. So one night, I told her
what they were saying: They are praying to a tiny girl on
the fifth floor. "Baba!" she said. She calls me Baba when
she doesn't believe me. She calls me Daddy when she
does. But that night I insisted they were praying to her. I
said they were praying she'd soon fall asleep—"Baba!"—
and then she would dream their lives for them. This si-
lenced her. She sat down on her child-sized wicker chair
and patted the grown-up chair beside her for me. I
obeyed. "They are very poor, aren't they?" she said. I
nodded. "Are we rich?" I told her I wasn't but her mother
was. A scold flashed across her features, but she relaxed
her usual vigilance against her parents' fights. "What do
they need?" she asked. I was puzzled. She said she'd
dream whatever they needed. I was reminded then of
the Armenian proverb: She sleeps for herself and dreams
for others. I said to her, they need you to fall asleep so
you'll dream. "Daddy," she said quietly. She yawned. She
was very tired, but she had to know one thing. "Can I
dream anything or do I have to dream only good things
for them?" This broke my heart. I carried her back to bed
and crawled in with her. I said I'd watch to make sure
her dreams were good. But I fell asleep.

Agitated, Safeyya asks Ib, "Please, would you do me the kind favor to read aloud what I have just written in your book?"

Ib says it would be his pleasure and sits upright, legs crossed. Ruqayyah pats his legs like a pillow and lays her head down, her beautiful eyes trained on him, with love, with that peculiar Egyptian look which says I don't know who you are but it's my right to stare at you. Ib is both deeply attracted to this woman on his lap and unsettled by her. It occurs to him that he probably should not read this story, but the momentum is now too strong. A distant tiny thud resounds, the cannon shot from the Citadel, signaling sunrise.

Safeyyah's story:

I am not a writer or an actor. I don't tell stories well. But Annahíd and I took the train to Luxor in January to see the Valley of the Kings. The train crashed in the middle of the night. She and I were like one being, crawling unhurt from the wreckage of our Pullman car. The fluorescent green lights of a mosque in a nearby village were the only illumination of our path, through a forest of

187

date palms. The mosque was five minutes away. Other lights from the town were concealed by the clumps of buildings, a tight fabric of homes and crisscrossing alleys that always look, from a distance, like one solid structure, planned and built with the whole in mind, when the actuality is warring parts, blood feuds, pathetic mud-brick walls that represent dozens of years of enmity, no matter what my father says of these places. The path we took meandered, because of the irregularly spaced trees, and rose and fell constantly, the earth registering the absence of trees gone centuries ago. Our group of survivors stumbled every few steps, voices cried out and swore in various European languages, bodies thumping against the hollow earth. Annahíd held my hand and reassured me and the strangers around us from time to time: "We're okay. The town people will know what to do." I did not share her optimism, but I loved Annahíd for this sweetness. Our small group of passengers had come together without deciding to, without speaking about it, by the accident of circumstance, which is the same motive behind most marriages. We groped for the village. When we finally arrived, we had grown accustomed to the steamy layers of darkness, so the festival lights of a small *mawlid* blinded us. We came around a high wall into the brightness and were immediately surrounded by chanting, swaying bodies. They were celebrating the birthday of their local saint. Our group of survivors, we discovered later, were all European tourists, except for Annahíd and me. This festival scared the Europeans more than the crash itself, or the ululations of the local women unleashed their terror, and the group sobbed as one, save Annahíd. She had the presence of mind to call out in French and then in English, "They will not hurt us. These are happy people. This is a good thing." In the light we saw our injuries and wounds and blood, and everyone grew strangely calm.

Ib lays his book on the sand. Gamal stands up, with Annahíd in his arms, and says, "She's really asleep now. I'll take her to bed." The sun, just above the horizon, is blinding and already hot. Squinting, Safeyya rises, and she and Gamal kiss on the lips, and they touch Annahíd's light brown hair. "I'll take her," Safeyya says gently, but Gamal walks away as if he has not heard his wife. Ruqayyah stumbles to her feet, picks up Ib's journal, and grabs Safeyya's hand. "I'll make dinner for you unbelievers at two o'clock in the afternoon," Ruqayyah says. She laughs briefly. She and Safeyya walk, arm in arm, following Gamal to the house.

Ib glances over at Charles, who has fallen asleep on a little hill of sand. Ib straightens and stretches. Off on the furthest visible ridge of desert to the south is a small caravan of camels being led, eventually, to the camel market in Imbaba, and likely to the slaughter-house after that. Nearer to the valley, a long delicate thread of electricity wires and ungainly towers break up the monotonous view. The camel drivers seem to prefer to stay as far from the encroaching urban civilization as possible, yet still remain in sight of it. The wind picks up, blowing brilliantly, and another dust storm is instantly upon them. Ib cannot see and plugs his ears with his fingers. He breaks for the grass and the house, remembers Charles, shouts his name, hears no response, then continues his sprint back to the green.